HORSE AND MULE TALES

Wes Warlick

iUniverse, Inc.
New York   Bloomington

Horse and Mule Tales

This is a work of fiction. All of the characters, names, incidents, organizations, and dialogue in this novel are either the products of the author's imagination or are used fictitiously.

iUniverse books may be ordered through booksellers or by contacting:

iUniverse
1663 Liberty Drive
Bloomington, IN 47403
www.iuniverse.com
1-800-Authors (1-800-288-4677)

ISBN: 978-1-4401-2268-2 (pbk)
ISBN: 978-1-4401-2269-9 (ebk)

Printed in the United States of America

iUniverse rev. date: 6/17/2009

I dedicate this book
To my wife Elaine who
put up with my cowboying,
mules and horses.

HORSE AND MULE TALES
First Cattle Drive, May, 1946

CHAPTER 1

I HAD RIDDEN MY BIKE OVER to Ed's house to collect my money on two horses I had taken to break for him. Bill was already there and Ed paid him his part for helping and paid me too. Just then, Big John drove up in his truck. He wanted to know if Ed and Bill would help drive about 250 cows from Port Acres to Port Arthur in two weeks, and said I was welcome to go, too. Big John was to pick us up at about 5 a.m. at Ed's house. My problem was I had to find something to ride. I got on my bike and started home about two miles away. I was nineteen years old and had never been on a cattle drive. I had a one-year-old buckskin colt at home, part Quarter horse, but he was too young to ride. My folks had bought a farm at Woodville, and on the farm was a black mule about 54" high named Jackson. Dad would plow with him sometimes and I had ridden him on the farm. I told my folks about the cattle drive and that I needed something to ride. I asked about going to Woodville and ride the mule back to Port Arthur. They thought the ride to Port Arthur would be a good experience for me and the cattle drive too. Dad said it was about seventy-five miles, and I couldn't ride Jackson too hard because he wasn't in good enough shape for 25 or 30 miles a day riding. I could ride maybe 15 or 20 and stop, feed him, and stake him out and let him graze on the side of the road. He told me to pack up what I might need and they would take me to Woodville tomorrow. For my bedroll, I took a blanket and folded it long ways. Then I got a large needle and string and sewed it up across the bottom and up the side about two feet. I figured I would sleep on one half and cover with the other half. I could put my feet in the pocket I had sewed up. Dad got a 6ft. by 8ft. tarp and said I could lie on half and cover with the other half.

1

I then got a change of clothes, gloves and I got my hunting knife. I put all this with my saddle so I would not forget it. I got an empty pill bottle and put five one dollar bills in it, and about six or seven aspirin. I put the pill bottle in my saddlebags. I got another pill bottle that was waterproof and put waterproof matches in it. The next thing I got was a thirty-foot rope and spliced a brass snap in each end. I then snapped a two-inch brass ring to one end and halter to the other end. Instead of trying to use a tree or post I would slide the ring up the rope and push the snap around a tree and snap it to the brass ring. I also tied my rain poncho on my saddle in case I was caught in a rain. Dad would never tell me what to do, he would just suggest it. He thought I should take a small hair brush to brush the mule with, because mules liked to be brushed every morning. It would be very important for the mule to like me since I would be depending on him to get me to Port Arthur. The next thing I got was about three or four gallons of feed for the next four days on the road. Then I put my hat and sun glasses in so I wouldn't forget them. I got a canteen I bought at a GI surplus store and filled it with water and I loaded all this in the car. I got a piece of paper and drew a map from Port Arthur to Woodville and all the towns in between. I marked all the creeks and a probable place to camp for the night. Next morning we left about 8 a.m., I wrote down the mileage on the car to figure about fifteen miles a day. Dad said it would be good to stop for the night every fifteen miles or so to let my mule rest and eat grass and feed. Eighteen miles from home was an auction barn, I told my folks I would plan on staying my last night there before getting home. Sixteen miles later was Pine Island Bayou, we slowed down and picked a spot to spend the night. Seventeen miles further we came to Village Creek.

We slowed down and I picked a spot to stop for the night there. The next place to stop would be about Warren, Texas. The miles would be about right and I saw a store I could buy something to eat. The next place would be the farm about two miles past Woodville. When we got to Woodville, dad stopped at a grocery store as he had another suggestion to make. He said we would go in the store and buy about six or eight carrots, that mules liked them and they would be a good reward for him when being handled. About a half mile from the store, there was a livestock sale barn and a horse shoer was there shoeing a horse. I asked dad to stop that I wanted to find out if he would shoe my mule and how much he charged. The man said that he would be there till about five o-clock and the fee was five dollars. I told him I would go get my mule and be back after a while. When we got to the farm dad said to take a carrot and hold it high so the mule could see it and call him into the lot and give him some feed also. While he was eating I shut the lot gate. After he finished eating I saddled him and rode back to the sale barn and had the mule shod for the long trip to Port Arthur. When he got through shoeing him I paid him and rode back to the farm to spend the night. The next morning I went out and gave the mule his carrot and then gave him some feed. While he was eating I went back in the house and ate breakfast. After breakfast I went to the lot and brushed the mule really good. I then saddled up and started on my first day of the trip to Port Arthur. My folks said they would stay around the farm two or three hours and would check with me on their way home.

I had ridden nearly four hours when they caught up with me. They stopped to see if I needed anything and to give me a sandwich. I told them I was ok and I would spend the night at Warren. Dad said to be careful and he would check on me in a day or so. I rode into Warren early in the afternoon. There was a grocery and feed store there. The owner was sitting on the front porch and invited me to sit down. I tied my mule to a tree so he could graze while I got something to eat. I sat down on the porch and we talked a while. I told him I was headed to Port Arthur and was looking for a place to stay the night. He said that he had about a three acre pasture all fenced in and I was welcome to turn my mule in there and he had an extra bed and it would be better than sleeping on the ground. I told him that was an offer I couldn't refuse and I would gladly accept. I bought some feed for my mule, fed him and turned him loose in the pasture. The store man was glad to have someone to visit with. We talked till about nine p.m.

The next morning I fed my mule his carrot and some feed. I ate breakfast with the store man, and then I brushed my mule, saddled up and hit the road again. The store man told me to stop by if I was ever up his way again. In the early afternoon I came to Kountze, Texas. I bought dinner for myself and rode on to Village Creek to camp for the night. I fed my mule and let him graze a while, then I moved him in to be close to me for the night. The next morning I gave my mule some feed, and then I brushed him good. I then saddled up and started on the road again. I made good time to Pine Island Bayou. There was a store there and I was ready to eat, so I bought six hot links and a package of hot dog buns. I rode a ways to the camp spot I saw on the way up, unsaddled my mule and tied him with a long rope so he could eat grass. I made camp by the bayou where others camped before, and I gathered firewood to cook my supper. I fixed my bedroll close to the fire. About dark I brought my mule in close to camp. I cooked three of the links on a stick and used three of the buns for supper. The next morning I cooked the last three links for breakfast. I had two buns left so I fed them to the mule. Afterwards I fed him his oats, I brushed him good, then saddled up and headed for the Beaumont Sale Barn. I got to Beaumont about noon and ate dinner at a cafe. I rode on through Beaumont and got to the sale barn about four. I knew the sale barn owner and he was there when I rode up on my mule. He remembered me as I had ridden a horse for him that he was selling at the barn. I told him I was headed for Port Arthur and I needed a place to stay tonight, and I had been on the road four days. He said I was welcome to stay there and to put my mule in a pen and to help myself to all the hay my mule could eat. His name was Tom Smith, everyone liked him. He said I could sleep on a couch in his office, and to make him and me at home would see me in the morning. I unsaddled my mule, brushed him and put him in a pen. I put all the hay I thought he might eat in the rack. I brought my saddle inside and called home to tell my folks where I was and about my trip and that I would be home the next day. I used the shower in his office then went to bed on his couch.

The next thing I knew it was daylight. I went to the pen to check on my mule, he was up and eating hay. Just then the owner drove up and asked how I slept last night. I told him I slept great and I sure thanked him for everything. He said I was welcome and to come back and use the barn when I needed too. We both walked next door to a cafe and I bought him and myself breakfast. I then went back to the barn and saddled my mule and hit the road to Port Arthur. About two hours later I saw dad waiting in the car on the side of the road. He asked how my trip was. I told him I had a good trip and was glad to be getting home.

We talked a while and he was glad to know I had a good trip. I got home about four p.m. that evening. I unsaddled the mule, brushed and fed him, then I opened the gate to a small pasture so he could graze a while. I let my mule rest till Sunday afternoon.

CHAPTER 2

I HAD BRUSHED AND FED JACKSON everyday. I figured he had gained about forty to fifty pounds. I saddled him and rode over to the roping pen where Ed, Bill and Randy were roping calves. When they saw me ride up on a mule, they kidded me about being a mule skinner. I just grinned; I had already decided that riding a mule wasn't as bad as I first thought. I told them I was going to ride Jackson on the cattle drive and I would be at Ed's house Saturday morning about 4:30 a.m. We all visited a while and I helped with the calf roping. I would ride up on Jackson and flag the roping when they were roping. After the roping, we all left. On the way home I figured I had five days to work with Jackson to teach him a few things.

The next morning I got an old tire and tied a rope to it to teach Jackson to pull with a saddle. After he got used to one tire, I added another tire and he took it in stride and pulled good. The next day I tried swinging a rope over his head. At first he spooked a little and I just talked to him and patted him on the neck and he settled down. By Friday I had Jackson pulling about three or four hundred pounds with a saddle horn. Saturday morning I got up at three a.m. I fed Jackson and ate breakfast. I filled my canteen and hit the road to Ed's house about three forty-five. As I rode along, I was thinking how much Jackson improved and always tried to do what I wanted. I had changed my way of thinking about mules. Mules are very smart, they like to check things out and make sure it is safe. I got to Ed's house at five a.m. Big John had just driven up. Ed was going to ride Santone and Bill was going to ride Booger. We put Santone in first, then Booger. I led Jackson up to the loading ramp, he saw the horses go in and he went right in. With three in the cab of the truck, there was no room for me, so I rode in the back of the truck. I knew not to stand by Booger, he might throw a fit. The safest one to stand by would be Jackson.

We got to Port Acres about six a.m. and they had just got the herd gathered. When they saw Jackson, they all started kidding me again about being a mule skinner, and to tie a lantern on his tail 'cause it would be dark when I got to Port Arthur. I just smiled, and went along with all of it. They put Jackson and me on a side of the herd with Roy. Roy had his three cow dogs with him. Two of the dogs were "drive dogs"; the other dog was a "catch dog". This dog just trotted a long beside Roy. We had driven the cows about a mile when a cow decided to leave the herd. She ran about forty yards and the two drive dogs were trying to turn her back. This catch dog that was with Roy was staying with him; he would look at the cow and then Roy. Roy would just look at the cow; the two drive dogs weren't having any luck getting the cow to go back to the herd. Then Roy told the catch dog to catch her. That dog ran out to the cow and grabbed her by the nose. He shook her good then let her go, the cow just kept fighting the dogs. Then the catch dog caught the cow again and shook her good. When the catch dog let her go he went straight for the middle of the herd. We had no more trouble with that cow for the rest of the drive. The catch dog came back and stayed with Roy.

About a mile down the road another cow left the herd and headed for the marsh. This cow got about forty feet from the road and bogged down up to her belly in the mud. We had to tie two lariat ropes together to have enough to reach the cow. One of the fellows got off his horse and waded out to the cow and roped her around the horns. Bill was riding Booger. Now, Booger is a good horse as long as everything goes ok. I figured that Bill or Ed would pull the cow out with their horse. Bill said that he had better not try to with Booger, that he might throw a fit. All the fellows said get the mule skinner to pull the cow out. They didn't know I had been teaching Jackson to pull with the saddle horn. I told them I would try and I wasn't sure that Jackson could pull the cow out of the mud. I took the rope and took two wraps around the saddle horn. I talked to Jackson and he got down low and pulled the cow all the way to dry land. Everyone was watching Jackson as he pulled the cow out. No one kidded me about my mule anymore. I was really proud of Jackson, and the more I rode him, the better I liked him.

All the rest of the drive everyone was looking at Jackson. We drove the herd straight to the intercoastal canal. There we turned east and drove them beside the canal till we got to the drawbridge. When we got there the bridge was up to let a tanker ship through. When they let the let the bridge down, we started driving thirty to forty cows at a time across the bridge. Some of the fellows would go across with the cows to hold them till all were across the bridge. When all were across we turned south and drove them to the gate and drove them in the pasture and the drive was over. Big John called all the fellows over to his truck. He had an ice chest full of beer for us to drink. I had tasted beer before, and I just didn't like it. I took it anyway and walked over to Jackson and told him he deserved the beer. I held it up high and put the bottle in his mouth. Jackson started drinking on the beer, and didn't stop until it was gone. Everyone agreed Jackson had earned that bottle of beer. Big John told us all thanks and for all of us to meet at his house the next morning for a big Bar-B-Que.

CHAPTER 3

I HAD BEEN RIDING JACKSON SINCE the cattle drive from Port Acres to Port Arthur. The more I rode this mule, the better I liked him. I had been out riding in an area. I like to know who has horses, which ones are good and which are not so good. Sooner or later, horses that are not good come up for sale. When I got home, I noticed my Uncle Jud sitting on the back porch talking to my mother. I unsaddled Jackson, brushed and fed him. Since I rode on the cattle drive Jackson had gained about fifty or sixty pounds, and was looking good. The first thing Uncle Jud asked me was if Jackson would work to a wagon, and I told him yes, and he would also pull with a saddle. Jud told me his workhorse was crippled and all he had to pull a wagon was his red mule, and he could sure use Jackson for about a month. Jud said he had about 30 acres of corn that was about ready to pull. He wanted to know if I would come up and help him out. This was on Friday, but I had a horse in the lot that sold and had to deliver him in the morning, so I said that I could leave here Monday or Tuesday. I probably could ride Jackson to Newton in about three or four days. Then my mother told me that we were going to take Jud home in the morning after I delivered the horse.

The next day when I got back home, I got about eight toe sacks out of the feed room. I figured we could use them some on the farm. I packed some extra clothes to take in the car, and save having to pack them on the back of the saddle. We took Uncle Jud to Newton Farm and came back home. I started packing the other things that I would need, the ones I had to take with me on Jackson. Sunday morning I figured I had just as well leave right after dinner and ride to the auction barn and spend the night there. The owner of the barn had told me I was welcome anytime I was traveling through. As I rode along the next day, I was thinking here I was making my second trip on Jackson. I was nineteen years old, had been buying and selling horses and mules for two years. When I got to the Beaumont sale barn it was about six o'clock in the evening. I put Jackson in one of the holding pens, fed him and went to a cafe and had supper. The next morning I fed Jackson and went back to the cafe for breakfast. While I was eating, Tom Smith, the owner of the sale barn, came in. I spoke to him and asked him to have a seat with me. He said that he had seen a mule in one of the pens, and had figured that he was mine. I told him I was headed to Newton to help my uncle pull about thirty acres of corn, and that I may find two or three horses to buy. Tom said he was headed for the other side of Silsbee to look at some cows and I could put my mule in his trailer and save some time in the saddle. I told him that it sounded good, and that I sure appreciated it.

When we got to Silsbee, it was the middle of the morning. I unloaded Jackson, thanked Tom and headed for Buna. It was late in the evening when I got there. I remembered that the rodeo grounds were on the edge of town and that would be a good place to spend the night. The next morning I rode on into Buna, found a cafe open, rode Jackson around to the back and tied him to a tree. After breakfast I headed for Kirbyville. That evening I met the owner of the auction barn at Kirbyville, and asked if I could put Jackson in one of his pens for the night. Also I asked if he knew of any saddle horses for sale. He told me that it was all right to put Jackson in a pen. I put him in a pen next to the outside where I would sleep with him that night. The next morning, I took Jackson out of the pen and got a horse brush that I always carried with me out of my pack. While I was brushing Jackson down, I looked up and saw a 1939 Ford pick-up with stake bed and pulling a trailer. I knew immediately it was my friend Clyde.

When I waved, he drove over to where I was. The first thing he asked was what I was doing there. I told him about Uncle Jud needing some help with the corn pulling, and that I may also find some horses for sale. Clyde said he was here to buy some fat calves to butcher, and that he too was looking for a good horse to work cattle on. I took him over and introduced him to the owner of the barn. He took us inside and showed us where to get our bid numbers. We went to the pens to look at livestock. I didn't see a good horse at all. Clyde saw some calves that would do for what the wanted. I told him we could go back to my mule and visit while I brushed and saddled Jackson.

While I was brushing Jackson, a fellow walked up and visited with us. We talked about Jackson, I said the more I rode him, the more I liked him. He wanted to know if I was interested in a good gentle gaited saddle mule. I said well it depends, I got a good mule right here, but I said I would take a look at his mule. He said the mule was at his farm in Bleakwood, which is about seven miles from where we were. I told him I was headed to Newton and I was going through Bleakwood and I would stop by and take a look at his mule. He said I should reach his farm in about 2 hours.

He said his name was Tom Parker, and that he owned "Parker's Store" in Bleakwood. He said the mule was in a pasture right by the store. I told him not to catch or saddle the mule, I wanted to see him do these things. When I got there the mule was in the pasture. He just called and the mule came up. Tom saddled the mule and he just stayed still. I asked him what the mules' name was and he said he called him Gray. Then he got on him and rode him and I was surprised at how smooth a ride Gray was. I rode him again and asked how much the mule cost. Tom said $150 for the mule, saddle, and tack. The saddle had adjustable stirrups and a good riding so I bought him. I also told Tom Parker I would be looking for 3 or 4 saddle horses. I told him how to get to Uncle Jud's farm, and that Uncle Jud didn't have a phone.

I decided to ride Gray to my Uncle Jud's farm. Jackson had to trot to keep up. I rode through Newton and on to the Jasper Highway. About one mile I turned left on a dirt road and rode about a mile to my uncle's 143 acre farm. He was on the front porch when I rode up. He said he knew it was I when he saw Jackson, and that he sure liked my Gray mule. I told him he was a saddle mule and wouldn't work to a wagon. I promised the man I bought him from that I would only use him under a saddle. The next morning we hooked up Jackson and Big Red, my uncles' mule, to the wagon. We packed the wagon full and were back at the house by 8:30. We started shucking corn and picking the silk off. Soon we had a dishpan full. Jud's wife (Aunt Willie) took the pan inside to the kitchen and started cutting corn off the cob.

Aunt Willie told me her niece was coming to help and she would be on the 1:00 p.m. bus. She asked me if I would go pick her up. I told her I didn't mind, but I didn't know her. She told me her name was Pam and that she would make a nameplate so Pam would find me. Uncle Jud and I shucked corn until about 11 a.m. and we stopped for a sandwich. Then I saddled up Gray Boy (as I was calling him now) and Jackson and left about 12:15 so I would have plenty of time to ride to Newton. I got to town and tied Gray Boy and Jackson in the back of the General Store, and went to the front and waited for the bus.

The bus was on time and about seven people got off. I held up my sign that had the name "Pam" written on it. Soon a pretty girl in her early twenties came up to me and said "Hello, I'm Pam." To my surprise, it was the girl who worked at the sale barn in Kirbyville. We both had a laugh and I told her my uncle didn't have a car so it was ride mule or wagon. She said she could ride a little bit. I took her to where Jackson and Gray Boy were tied. When she mounted Jackson, I knew she had done some riding before. When we got to the farm I unsaddled Gray Boy and Pam unsaddled Jackson. We put the saddles in the tack room across the hall from the corncrib, then turned Gray Boy and Jackson out in the pasture. We shucked corn and canned corn until about 6 p.m. The next morning we still had lots of corn on the porch. So Uncle Ed started shucking corn. Pam and I hooked up Jackson and Big Red to the wagon and went to the field and brought in a load of corn.

We put about half on the porch and half in the corncrib. The next day was Saturday, and Uncle Jud thought we needed to rest from the corn pulling, but we needed some groceries and fruit jars. He told Pam and me, if we wanted to, we could take the wagon and go to town and get some supplies. Uncle Jud also told me to call my folks and tell them to come up and get some corn, and also to find out what day they would be here. When we got to town, I called home and they said they would be up Tuesday morning. I asked them to bring two or three changes of clothes. We bought groceries and four cases of pint fruit jars. While we were in town I saw Tom Parker, he told me he had a good horse at a good price. He said it would work or ride and that he had a running walk and was very gentle. The horse was a red roan, about fourteen hands high, and six years old. Tom told me the man that owned him was getting out of the horse business and wanted to sell the horse, saddle, and all tack, and that he was at his store. We told Tom as soon as Pam and I could get back to the farm and unload the supplies, we would saddle Gray Boy and Jackson and we would be at his store around three or four o'clock.

We got to the farm and Pam and Uncle Jud unloaded supplies while I saddled Jackson and Gray Boy. We were at Toms store by three. Pam wanted to put the saddle on the roan because it had adjustable stirrups on it. The roan stood still to saddle and Pam got on him and rode him. He quickly hit a fast running walk. Pam smiled and nodded her head. I asked Tom how much he wanted for all of it. He told me one hundred and thirty dollars for everything. I paid him and put the saddle that came with the roan on Jackson. Tom thanked me and I thanked him, I told him to let me know if he got anymore-good horses. We headed for the farm and Gray Boy and the roan hit a good running walk all the way to the farm. The next day was Sunday, and we sat around all morning. After dinner, Pam wanted to go riding. I asked Uncle Jud about the property adjoining to the farm. He said it belonged to a timber company, and there were logging roads all over it. We rode about three hours and I was really pleased with buying the roan. He was the type of horse that I liked to have about eight or ten of in my pasture. Monday, Pam and I pulled another load of corn, and while we were in the cornfield a man came to the farm and bought the last twenty acres of corn. We had about one more load of corn to pull on the first ten acres.

My folks came up the next day and I asked my dad if he would like to drive a good team of mules. He said yes very quickly. While I hooked up Big Red and Jackson, dad told me he was going to buy a two wheeled garden tractor, and that if I wanted to sell Jackson to go ahead because he would not need him anymore. I told him I wouldn't have any problem selling him. We pulled the last load of corn and put all but three toe sacks in the corn crib for feed. I saved about four feed sacks for traveling. I asked my folks if they would mind giving Pam a ride to Kirbyville, and that Uncle Jud had given Pam and I each a case of corn. It would be hard to pack two cases of corn on Jackson with the feed corn I was packing. They said sure, and that they didn't mind at all. I told my folks I would leave out the next morning and would see Pam at the sale barn on Wednesday.

I got up the next morning and saddled up Gray Boy, Roan, and Jackson. I put about half a toe sack of corn on each side of Jackson for feed on the way back home. I got to Kirbyville Sale Barn about noon. I tied up my stock at the same place, and then went inside and said hello to Pam. I told Pam that I didn't see any horses or mules that I wanted to take back home, and that I was going to go ahead and leave. I gave her my address and phone number and told her to write me and keep a look out for some mules and horses.

I tightened up the saddles on all three horses and was about ready to leave. Just then, a man drove up with a sorrel pony with a flax mane and tail. The man came over to see if I was looking for a good gentle pony because h is daughter had already outgrown the horse and he was trying to sell it. He needed to sell the horse and the saddle because she wanted a barrel horse to take to rodeos. I told him I had the three horses and really didn't need anymore, (as soon as I saw the horse, I knew I wanted to buy him). I asked the man how much he wanted for the horse and saddle. He said that the horse was kid gentle, didn't kick, was easy kept, and easy to catch. He said that he wanted eighty dollars for the horse and saddle. I told him I couldn't pay that, but I would give sixty dollars for all. He said he would think about it and he led the pony around trying to get more money. I untied my stock, got on Gray and started for Buna. The man waved me down and said he was offered fifty dollars and he would the take the sixty I offered him if I sill wanted to trade. I gave him sixty dollars and tied the horse to Jackson and headed for Buna. I decided I'd call the pony Dan. He looked like a small Belgian horse. I rode steady and got to Buna at about six o'clock. I stopped at a cafe and ate supper. Then I went to the rodeo grounds to spend the night. The next morning, I staked all of the stock outside and let them graze.

I saddled up and headed for Silsbee. I crossed the river about noon and stopped at a store for a bite to eat. Right after I left the store, a pickup came by. It went about a hundred yards and quit running and coasted to a stop so I rode up to the truck. There was a lady and two boys in the truck. One boy was about ten and one about seven. I asked if I could help and she said she thought the truck was out of gas. I asked how far she was going, and she said that she was only about two miles away from home. I told her I could tow her home and asked if her ten year old could ride. She said he could ride and that they had a horse at home. He said his name was Joe and his brother's name was David. I put Joe on Dan. Then I lead the roan to the front of the truck and tied a rope to the bumper. I told the lady to turn the key off and to put the truck in neutral. I gave Joe the lead rope on Jackson and to tell him to lead the way to his house. It took about thirty minutes to get there. Joe's daddy was on the front porch waiting for them to come home. His name was Bob Taylor and he was really glad to see us. Joe was riding Dan as proudly as he could be. I rode Gray Boy and lead the roan as he pulled the truck to the back where the gas tank was.

Bob introduced himself and was really glad to know that his family didn't have to sit on the side of the road. I took the lead rope off Jackson and tied him to Roan and untied the truck. Joe asked if he could ride Dan a little more. I told him sure, and then David came running up and wanted to ride too. I told him that he could ride also, and that he was really gentle. I lead the roan around in the lot to see if I thought David would be OK riding by himself. I looked back toward the house and saw Bob talking to his wife. I saw David would be ok riding the roan by himself, and let them both out into a small pasture. I let the boys trade horses and they liked this trade. Soon Bob came walking up and asked me if I was in a hurry to leave, because they wanted me to stay for supper. I said that I would stay, and that I had some corn on the cob and that I had plenty if they would like some to go with supper. Bob said that would be good, and that they hadn't had fresh corn in a long while.

Bob kept watching his boys riding Dan and Roan. In a bit he asked if the horses were for sale and trade. I told him I would like to see his boys with good horses and I would try to work something out that we could both live with. Bob told me his Dun horse was gentle and didn't kick or buck, but it wasn't a kid horse. He said he would like to trade that horse (Chico) in on both my horses. He said that he had done some calf roping on Chico and he was too fast for his boys. Bob said that he wanted to keep his saddle, but he would need the saddle that was on Dan. I told Bob I would trade for one hundred dollars difference. He said that sounded fine to him. When the boys rode up to the barn, Bob told them of the trade. They both were happy they each had a horse to ride. After supper, Joe and David asked if they could ride some more.

Bob and Mrs. Taylor asked me to spend the night because it was too late to spend the night on the road. I told them thanks and that I would sleep in the barn so I'd hear if they had any problems. Bob said they had a screened in porch and iron cot and that I could hear if anything went on at the barn. I agreed with that and we sat around and talked till bedtime.

I woke up about daylight but not before Joe and David. We all went to the barn and started brushing our horses and mules. In a bit, Bob came into the barn and paid me the hundred dollars and thanked me for everything. He told me there was a gate at the back of the pasture and the dirt road went to Silsbee and there would be less traffic. He asked if Joe and David could ride a ways and he and Mrs. Taylor would follow in their pickup. I told them sure; it would be a good experience for them. Bob told me thanks and if I was this way again I was welcome to stay, and if they weren't home, I could still use their barn and pens. I saddled Gray Boy, put a lead rope on Chico and tied Jackson to Chico. Bob and Mrs. Taylor drove ahead in the pickup and had the gate open when we got there. We rode along and talked for about two hours, and then Bob stopped us and told us that they had better head back to their house. We all said our good-byes and Bob told me to stop by any time. I rode steady and got to the Beaumont Sale Barn that evening. Tom Smith was still at the barn and wanted to know how my trip was. I told him I had a good trip and I had my friend Clyde a good horse if he was still interested in one.

Tom asked about Jackson, he said he knew a fellow that wanted a good mule if I would sell him. I told him I had talked to my dad and he was going to buy a two-wheel tractor to garden with and wouldn't need Jackson and I could sell him if I wanted to. Tom asked how much for Jackson. I told him two hundred and fifty dollars for the mule, saddle, and bridle. In a few minutes Tom came back out and said that the man would be there in a few minutes to look at Jackson. I called Clyde on the phone and told him about Chico. Clyde told me he would want Chico, but he had sold his saddle and would need one. I told him I had a good saddle I would sell him.

Clyde said he needed the horse and saddle early in the morning. He had to help Tony catch some cows. I told him I was at the sale barn and would wait for him. Clyde said he would be there about daylight the next morning. I then called my folks and told them I would be home about noon. Later on, a man drove up to look at Jackson. He rode Jackson around a little and said he would take him. He said he was going on a pack trip in Colorado, and that it was a mule only ride. He would be back in the morning about seven to pick him up. He said his name was T. Walker, and he would like to ride along and camp if I didn't mind. I told him I was going back to Kirbyville in about 10 days and would try to pick up some mules to sell. I told him I would call him after I had all the mules and horses I needed. It would probably be on a Tuesday night when I would call and tell him where to meet me. The next morning Clyde drove up at about daylight. I had Chico saddled and ready to go. He rode him a little and said he wanted the horse, saddle and all, and then loaded him into the trailer. Clyde hadn't been gone long when T. Walker drove up. He loaded up Jackson and said he would be waiting for my call. I saddled up Gray Boy and headed for home. I got home about noon and put Gray Boy in the lot and turned him loose.

CHAPTER 4

My uncle Jud came by one day and told me about a shutdown job at the Atlantic Refinery. He could get me a job there if I wanted it. It would last about two weeks and I could make some good money. After the job and I told my uncle I was going to Kirbyville soon to buy some horses and mules. Jud said to come on up to his farm in Newton. He would know if there were any horses or mules for sale. The next Tuesday morning about eight a.m. the phone rang and it was Pam in Kirbyville. She told me there were a good buckskin horse and a saddle there to be sold at the Wednesday sale. I told Pam I would be there Wednesday morning, and I thanked her for calling. I then called Tom Smith to see if he was headed in the Kirbyville area because my mule and I needed a ride. Tom told me he was going that way and I was welcome to go with him. We would leave about eight a.m. on Wednesday. I told him I would ride my mule to the sale barn Tuesday and spend the night there. I then called Parker's Store in Bleakwood. I told Mr. Parker I would be up his way on Thursday. He said he had a big gray mare mule that I might like. I left about one p.m. and headed Gray Boy toward Beaumont. He hit a good gait and we made good time all the way. I put him in the same pen that he was used to. I gave him some feed and hay, and put my saddle and duffel bag in a tack room and went over to the cafe to eat supper. Tom was there and waved me over to his table. He said he was headed to Kirbyville to buy roping calves. He wanted to know if I would buy some calves for him, and said that he would go on to Center, Texas and buy there. Both sales were on Wednesday. I told him that I would try, but I would buy calves on his number and mules on my number. Tom said he would be there about seven a.m. to eat breakfast and load my mule. I slept in the tack room that night. About daylight I got up and fed Gray Boy, went back and packed my bedroll, and went over to the cafe. Soon Tom came in and we had breakfast. Then we went to the barn and I saddled my mule, put my bedroll in the truck, loaded my mule and headed for Kirbyville. We got there about 9:30 a.m. and met the new owner of the sale barn, Mr. Porter. Tom told him I would be buying for him, and he would be back later to pick up what I had bought. Tom left for Center and I went back to the pens to see what was there. In a few minutes, Pam walked up. She showed me the buckskin horse. This horse was about six years old. She then showed me the saddle and tack that was to be sold. I told Pam I would try to buy the horse saddle. She then showed me a big donkey gelding that was going through the sale, including an army saddle that went with him. Later on a man brought in a sorrel mule with a flax mane and tail. He said the mule would work and ride. I told the man I would like to ride the mule and see how I liked him. The mule rode well, and I asked the man what the mules name was. The man told me the mules name was Rusty.

When the sale started they sold saddles and tack first. I bought the saddle and tack that Pam showed me that went with the buckskin horse. I paid forty dollars for the saddle. I bought Smokey for sixty dollars and bought the mule, Rusty, for fifty dollars. I bought the donkey and the army saddle for twenty-five dollars. Later, Pam wanted to know if I was going to Newton because she wanted to go along and visit her Aunt Willie. I told Pam that she was welcome to come with me, and that she could ride Smokey. Pam finished her work at the sale barn on Thursday morning. I had Gray Boy and Smokey saddled and we headed for Bleakwood. I led Pedro the donkey and Rusty, the red mule. Mr. Parker was waiting for us when we got there. He showed us the big gray mare mule. The mule was over fifteen hands high, and had big feet. Mr. Parker said she would work and ride and was kid gentle. I bought the mule and the rest of the sack of feed Mr. Parker had been feeding. I paid him sixty dollars for all of it. I was leading Rusty, and Pedro the big donkey. Pam said she would lead Dolly, the draft mule.

Mr. Parker was glad to see Gray Boy. He walked over to him, and began to talk to him and pet him. Gray Boy knew him, and I could tell he was gad to see him. We visited for a while, and I told him to let me knew if he got any more horses and mules. We then headed for

Newton. We stopped at the General Store there. I went in and bought a canned ham and some other supplies to help out at the farm. Uncle Jud was sitting on the front porch when we started up the lane. When he saw my red mule he wanted to know all about him. He had bought a gray roan mule to go with Big Red, but when he saw Rusty he said that would make him a good pair. Uncle Jud wanted to know if I would trade Rusty for his Gray Roan Mule. I told him my mule was bigger than his mule and I would trade for one hundred dollars more. I laughed and he laughed, then he said, "Looks like I taught you to be a good a mule trader." Then I told him I would trade even. He said that was ok with him.

Pam took the groceries to her Aunt Willie and Uncle Jud while I unsaddled the horse and mules. Uncle Jud put Rusty with Big Red (he wanted to see how they got along together). Then he started talking about Dolly, the big gray mare mule. I told him all I knew about Dolly. He told me about a black mule that was for sale, gentle to work and ride. The only thing wrong was they couldn't catch him. The price for the mule is ten dollars. He told me that he knew a way that might work to catch the mule. The mule was in a fifty-acre pasture. We could take the Big Gray Mule over there and put a belt around her neck and tie a small bell to it. Mules will usually take to a gray mare and follow them anywhere. I told him it would be worth a try. He said he would go over to the man's house and see if the mule was for sale. I called Dolly and they all came into the lot. I caught Dolly and Sandy, the gray roan mule. I figured I might as well try him to see how he rode. Uncle Jud was back soon and said the mule was still for sale. He told me to go to the highway and go north and he would drive the truck and wait for me at a certain dirt road.

Uncle Jud had bought a truck after working the shutdown because he thought it would be better than driving the wagon and mules. When we got to the pasture Uncle Jud opened the gate. He put the bell on the gray mule's neck and turned her loose. We then went back to the farm. I rode Sandy back and was real happy the way he rode. He was not gated, but he had a good running walk. The next day I had put my saddle and tack in the back of the truck we went back to the pasture. When we got to the pasture I called Dolly and shook the feed bucket. Dolly headed for the pen with the Mule right behind. They went in and I put feed in the trough, and Uncle Jud shut the gate. When the mule saw he had no placed to go, he let me walk up to him and put on the bridle. Then I caught Dolly and saddled her. I led the mule and Uncle Jud went to pay the man for the black mule. The man told Uncle Jud that the black mules name was Koko. Uncle Jud was waiting for the mules and me when I got to the farm. He told me not to turn Koko loose just yet because he wanted to school him on being caught. He went in the barn and got a chain about eight feet long, and fastened it to KoKo's front foot. We then turned Koko out to a pasture by himself.

Later that evening we walked out to where he was. We got around him to drive him to the pen. When he saw we wanted to catch him, he broke to run the other way. Koko ran about sixty or seventy feet when the chain wrapped up his front feet. He rolled two complete times, jumped up and ran again. The chain wrapped his front feet again, but Koko stopped before he fell. Koko then walked all the way to the pen. After dinner Pam and I decided to take Sandy and Koko for a ride on a logging road at the back of the farm. While we were gone Mr. Parker drove up to my uncle's house. He told Uncle Jud he needed to talk to me. Uncle Jud and I had a signal we used. Jud blew Mr. Parker's horn, one long and two short. I heard the signal and we headed back to the farmhouse. In a few minutes we rode up. Mr. Parker walked up; to meet us, and said he had a man in the truck with a problem. His son was visiting some folks about twenty miles from his store and the last rain had washed out the bridge on Highway 87. The road was dirt from Call, Texas to Deweyville, Texas. The heavy rain had the road so bad you could not drive a truck down it, and with the bridge out, he needed to hire someone with mules or horses to take him and his son back to Parker's store.

About this time the man in the truck came over and Mr. Parker introduced us. He was Ed Brown, a man over six feet tall and over two hundred pounds. I ask him when he needed to go after his son and exactly how for was it. I also wanted to know if he had ever ridden a mule before. He said he had but it had been a long time. Mr. Brown said that it was about twenty miles, and that he would like to go in the morning. He also wanted to know if we could make it there and back in one day. I told him Pam and the mules and I could. I then ask how old the boy was, and had he ever ridden. He told me his son was twelve, and he could ride well. The boys' name was Mike, and I figured he would do just fine. So I told Mr. Brown that we could probably make the trip in one day. I took Mr. Brown over to the lot and showed him Dolly the mule he would be riding. I then showed him the mule I would be riding, and the one that Pam was going to ride. Ed asked if we could bring another mule so we could pack in groceries. He knew his folks had not been able to get out for supplies. I told him I could bring Koko along and that would be two pack mules to pack in supplies. Ed then asked how much all of this was going to cost. I figured for the trip there and back would run eighty dollars. That was fine with Ed. So I said that we would leave Parker's store at daybreak in the morning. We would have the supplies in four sacks not over sixty pounds each, and that we could put two sacks each on Koko and Sandy. I asked Uncle Jud if we could use his saddle and if he still had the old saddle without stirrups. He said he did, but we needed to check the old saddle. We checked it out, cleaned and oiled it, and put my long girt on it.

The next morning we got up early, fed all the stock, and ate breakfast. Aunt Willie made us four sandwiches for us to have to eat on the way back. After breakfast we saddled up and headed for Parker's Store. Pam took the lead rope on Dolly, and I took the lead rope on Koko and tied it to the neck of Sandy. I took Sandy's lead rope and got on Gray Boy. We got to Parker's Store about daylight. Ed Brown was ready and waiting on us. He had bought some hunting pants, a shirt, and a cap. I tied the sacks of groceries on Sandy and Koko. Ed got on Dolly, Pam took Koko and we left for the twenty-mile trip. Ed told me his grandfather had bought this place about 1900, that he got a clear title to 1280 acres. His grandfather named the place Sportsman Lodge. The land started at Highway 87 and went to the Sabine River. He told me that there was a natural lake about 100 yards wide and one mile long. The lake is good fishing and duck hunting. There's good squirrel hunting and deer hunting. His father charges people to hunt and fish. He had four cabins if they want. The lodge has a good business when the road is not to muddy.

We soon came to Call, Texas. We rode on through about five miles we came to a creek. The bridge was still there but the dirt was washed out at the bridge. We went down to the creek and crossed there, the water was about two feet deep. This is why I didn't bring Pedro; donkeys don't like to cross-creeks. We made good time and soon came to the big creek that had washed out the bridge. The bridge was one hundred feet out in the pasture from the road. We crossed the creek on the side where the bridge used to be. The water was bout three feet deep. We didn't have any trouble. About 10:30, we came to a road, it had a sign that read SPORTSMAN LODGE TWO MILES. Ed had to phone his folks from Parker's Store and they were looking for us. They were sure glad to get the supplies we packed in. Ed introduced us to his folks and to his son, Mike. Mike was surprised to see us ride in on mules and one horse. He wanted to know which mule he would ride. I told him he would take Sandy. The saddle on Koko didn't have any stirrups so I used it for a packsaddle. Pam helped Mrs. Brown put up groceries and Mike and I brought the groceries in. Ed visited with his dad. I had Mike get on Sandy; I wanted to see if the stirrups were the right length. Ed told his folks good-bye and if they needed anything to let him know and he would call when they got home.

We left out about one p.m. When we got to the creek where the bridge had washed out, we stopped to rest and show Mike what happened to the bridge. Ed looked at where the bridge had been and said he didn't think it could be ready for travel in thirty days. They would need more supplies brought in. Mike quickly said if we took supplies in that he wanted to go. We crossed the creek and as we rode along, Ed asked me what I thought about a trip back to Sportsman Lodge about the first week in September and would I be available. I looked at Pam and she nodded her head, I then told Ed I would keep that weekend open and let him know. Ed told me he had a ten-year-old son at home, and his wife could ride and so it probably would be four of them. He wanted to know what it would cost to make the two-day trip. We could use the four cabins his dad has at the Sportsman Lodge. I told Ed I would let him know when we got to Parker's store. As I rode along with Pam, we talked about all the things we would need. We knew we would need six riding mules and two or three pack mules, and we would need saddles for everything. I figured five dollars a day for the horses, mules, and tack. Pam said she would go for fifteen dollars a day. When we got to Parker's store I told Ed for the two-day trip, it would cost one hundred eighty dollars. He said that was fine with him and it would be a good weekend for his family. I told Ed he might rent one of Mr. Parker's cabins and come up on Friday before.

When they got there, Pam and I would be at my uncle's farm and they could come by and let us know they were here. We said good-by at Parker's Store and Pam and I left for my uncle's farm. We got there just before dark. The next morning I told Uncle Jud all about the trip and that we were planning another trip the first weekend in September. I asked if I could rent his two mules and saddles, and would he sell me that old saddle that had no stirrups. Uncle Jud told me that I could count on the saddle and two mules, and I could have the old saddle with no stirrups. It had been there when he bought the farm. He also told me I could leave Smokey here, that he had plenty of feed and that he would already be there. I said all right and we would be back in about ten days to about two weeks to buy more mules. I would need eight or nine head, six for riding and two or three for packing.

We visited the weekend and left Monday morning for Kirbyville. I left Smokey at Jud's farm, Pam rode Sandy, and I rode Gray Boy and led Dolly width Koko tied to her and Pedro tied to Koko. When we got to Parker's Store I called J. Walker and told him I was headed back for Kirbyville, and if he still wanted to ride with me to come up to the sale barn. He said he wanted to and his brother and G.T. Stafford wanted to come along and did I have any mules for sale. I said that they were welcome to come along, and that I had two mules about the size of Jackson, but that they needed to bring their saddles. Before leaving Parker's Store, I told Tom about our nest trip, packing supplies to Sportsman Lodge. Tom said Ed had already told him and that he would be looking for us. I told him I figured on three pack mules if I could find them, and that we would be back in about two weeks. Pam and I headed for Kirbyville.

The next morning T. Walker, his brother J. and G.T. Stafford got there about ten. As soon as they saw Koko, T. Walker wanted him, and G.T. wanted Sandy. They had Jackson in a new sixteen-foot horse trailer. G.T. hadn't brought his saddle; it had been left behind in Dallas. The three of them were going to Colorado on an all mule trail ride the last week in September. The next morning we all headed for Buna. Pam stayed in Kirbyville; she had to work the sale the next day. T. Walker said he would drive the truck and GT could use his saddle on Sandy. I told him we would make camp at the rodeo grounds in Buna that night. We had a good ride to Buna and didn't have any trouble.

While we were unsaddling our mules and staking them out to graze, I saw a pick-up truck drive up. I knew it was Bob Taylor. I made the introductions to all the fellows. Bob ask if we were headed to Silsbee. I told him yes we would be leaving in the morning. Bob said his boys were out of school, it was a teachers meeting, and said that the boys really enjoyed riding to Silsbee. He then asks if the boys could ride along with us. I told him sure, and that if he wanted to ride that he could ride Pedro but all I had for him was an old army saddle. I told him we would be by his house about nine in the morning. When we got to the Taylor's the next morning, they were all ready. I told Bob we would ride to the back gate like we had done before. The boys rode through the pasture, and Bob and his wife drove the pick-up. Bob liked my idea about riding Pedro. And it seemed a good time to ride with his boys, so that is what he did. His wife said that she would meet us in Silsbee about four p.m. As we rode along Bob and I talked. I told him his boys could spend the night camped with us. I also said that he could too, or go home with his wife and come back for the boys in the morning. I said if he wanted to he could ride Pedro back with the boys and I would be back in about ten days to get Pedro, or he could just keep him until I needed him. Bob liked the idea and thanked me. He decided to go home for the night and return in the morning. The next day they were there before we got saddled. The Taylor's headed home and the rest of us headed for Beaumont.

When we got to the sale barn that evening, Tom Smith was still there. When he saw the big gray mule, he told me that he knew a fellow that was looking for a mule about that size if I wanted to sell. I said that the mule was a little big for me and that I might sell. He called the man and told him about Dolly. The man had a gray mule at home about the same size, and that they would make a good pair. He said that he had a saddle horse and would I take a trade in. I told him to bring the horse and his saddle and I would try to trade. The next morning he got to the sale barn about eight. The horse was a dark Palomino, half fox-trotter, one-quarter Belgian, and a quarter Arabian. The man told me the horses name was Nugget; he was a good Fox-Trotter, and kid gentle. I put the saddle on him and rode him around. He had a good gait and traveled well. I told the man that I would trade with him for fifty dollars. The man thought that was a good trade so the deal was done.

I called home and told my folks I was at the sale barn in Beaumont and headed home. They told me to meet them in Nederland, that they had some good news. When I got to Nederland they met me and showed me a house with twelve acres and barn with pens. The man that owned the place wanted to trade his place for the farm in Woodville. My dad said that all he wanted was the house and two acres, and he thought I might want the barn and the other ten acres. Dad also said that he would talk to the bank and help me get a loan. I put my mules in the pasture and waited for the bank to open on Monday.

Monday morning I went to the bank with my dad and Mr. Todd who owned the land, and got a loan and signed the papers. Moving to Nederland would give me more room to train mules and horses. It was also a lot closer to the sale barn. We got moved in by Thursday. I had a big barn for my stock and a cabin to put my things in. Joe Clark called and said that he needed mules broke for ridding and for working. I saddled Gray Boy and led Nugget to Joe's place to see what he had. When I got there, he had a pair of black mules, and one sorrel mule. He wanted to trade the sorrel mule for training the black mules to ride and work. The black mules were only halter broken. He had harnesses and tack, so I told him it would take about four or five weeks to train them right. I told Joe that I would take the sorrel mule as partial payment, but that it would cost him one hundred dollars each to train the black mules. I said that I would take the mules to my uncles' place in Newton to train them. When I brought them home they would both ride and work. Joe said that that would be fine; he knew I would train the mules right. Joe told me the sorrel had a star in his forehead so he named him Star, but he had not named the black mules yet. I told him for now I would just call them number two and number three mules.

I led Nugget in the lot and tied the lead rope on Star to Nugget. I then tied number three to Star, and number two to number three. I then put the collar and harness on number two and three. If they were going to act up, Nugget would help calm them down. By the time I got home the mules were trailing well. I put the mules in the lot, and then took one at a time and started brushing them and talking to them. I worked with the mules all weekend. I told my folks that I was going to take the mules to Newton on Monday to teach them to work and ride. I said that I would be gone about a month and that I was going to pack in the supplies to the Sportsman Lodge.

I saddled Gray Boy and Nugget and put an old saddle on Star that I had fixed from one that didn't have any stirrups. I saddled the number two mules with broken tree saddle and put the collar and harness on. I put another saddle on the number three mules, put the collar and harness on and tied them to the saddle. I left for Silsbee about nine in the morning, rode hard and got to the general store about four that afternoon. I unsaddled everyone and put him and her in separate pens. I bought a sack of feed and fed all of them good. I kept out enough feed for the morning, and divided the rest into four. I put this feed in four toe-sacks to put on the number three and number two mules to carry. The next morning, Tuesday, I saddled up and headed for a long ride to Kirbyville. I didn't think I would need Pedro, so I left him with the Taylor's till I came back. I rode hard to train the mules to pack. It was just dark when I got to the Kirbyville sale barn. I put the mules in pens and went to tell Pam that I was back.

The next morning I fed the mules real good and took Pam out to breakfast. By the time we got back the stock had finished eating. Pam saddled Gray Boy and Nugget while I saddled Star and the two black mules. The two days of hard riding had already got them well under control. We headed for Parker's Store. As we rode along, Pam asked if all I did was to trade mules and horses. I told her I worked some at the sale barn in Beaumont, and had been competing in rodeos for about two years. I rode in saddle-bronc and bareback, and usually won money in both events.

We soon got to Parker's Store and stopped to say hello. Tom told us that Ed Brown had called and he had bought his boys each a saddle, and was still planning on the trip. I said that was good because I was short on saddles. I told Tom that Ed would probably call again to see if we were here. We then left for my uncle's farm. When we rode up he was surprised at all the mules I had. I told him about the deal I had made on #2 and #3. He liked the deal on the mules. We could hook them to Big Red and Rusty and plow the field. The fellow that bought the twenty acres of corn was going to want about forty acres of corn. My uncle told me he would need about ten acres of corn for feed and to can some for the house. Also he wanted to plant about two or three acres of sweet potatoes. He wanted to plow and disk all of this to help kill the weeds. By the time we got all of this done, the mules would be well broke to work. We could work them in the mornings and ride them in the evenings. By the time it came to the weekend to make the pack trip to Sportsman Lodge, the mules were well broke to work and ride.

Friday evening, Ed and his family drove up to the farm. He introduced us to his wife and to Pat his ten year old. Ed showed me the saddles he had bought, so I said lets go ahead and try the saddles on Smokey and Nugget to see if the stirrups were the right length. The boys got on and rode around and everything was fine. I told Ed we would be at Parker's Store about sunrise in the morning. He said that would be fine. The next morning we left the farm and got to Parker's Store just at the sun was rising. We loaded #2 and #3 mules with Groceries and put some behind the saddle of Nugget and Smokey. I put Ed on Big Red, his wife on Rusty, Pat on Nugget, Mike on Smokey, and Pam on Star and I rode Gray Boy. I led #2 mule and Pam led #3 mule. I tied the packs on good and we left for Sportsman Lodge. Ed and his wife up front and the boys next, Pam and I rode in the back. The bridge was still out so we crossed the creek, the water was down and we had no trouble. We got to Sportsman Lodge about noon. Ed's Folks were sure glad to see us. I told Ed to visit with his dad while I unpacked and Pat and Mike could haul the supplies in. After I got this done, I took the mules and horses and turned them loose in about a ten-acre pasture. We put Pat and Mike's bedroll in the first cabin, Ed and his wife's bedroll in the next cabin, Pam's things in the third cabin, and I took the last cabin.

The next morning Pat and Mike wanted to ride around at the lodge. I told them sure and we went and caught Nugget and Smokey. They rode for about two hours, never out of sight long. After dinner, Pam, Pat, Mike, and I caught the mules and got ready for the trip. I noticed Ed and his wife talking. Then Ed walked over to us and asked if I would sell Smokey and Nugget and if so they would leave them here. I told him yes, I would take three hundred for both horses. Ed said that was fine and to unsaddle them and put them in the pasture. I put pat on Gray Boy and Mike on Star. Pam and I rode the pack mules. We made good time back to Parker's Store. Ed told me how much the enjoyed the trip and wanted to do it again. Ed wrote me a check for everything. Pam quickly got off #3 mule and got on Star, she commented I sure like a gaited mule better. I got on Gray Boy and we led the mules to the farm. As we rode along, Pam wanted to know if she could buy Star. She said she would put her earnings on a down payment and she could ride Star to the farm when she got off at the sale barn. I told Pam that she had helped a lot breaking and packing to the lodge and I figured she had earned Star and he was hers.

Pam was delighted and smiled all the way to the farm. We got to the farm before dark. My uncle was waiting for us. He helped us with the mules and feeding. I paid him for using his saddle and mules, and tried to pay him for helping training #2 and #3 mules. He said no that he got the cornfield laid by and that helped him a lot, and I could come back in the spring and help plant corn and sweet potatoes. I told him I would be there and I might bring some more mules. The next day we were all setting on the porch talking. My uncle told me he was going to the Nederland area and was going to work shutdowns at some of the refiners. He said he could make some good money and he could get me a job too. I told him the mule and horse business would be dead till March, and I needed to work I had notes to meet on the ten acres. I told him I had an office building that came with the land and he could stay in it. It is about sixteen by thirty-two, it has a bathroom with a shower, and a hot water, sink and iron bed, a two burner electric hot plate, and all he had to bring was sheets and a bed cover. Pam told us she could ride Star to the farm when she got off on Thursday and stay with Aunt Willie till Tuesday and help take care of Big Red and Rusty. Aunt Willie liked that idea as she wouldn't be all by herself.

The next morning, Pam and I left for Kirbyville. I packed everything on #2 and #3 mules. We got to the Parker's Store and stopped to say hello and I bought a sack of feed. I divided the feed and tied it on the mules. I told Tom I probably wouldn't be back till March, that I'd be back then to help my uncle do some planting. We got to the sale barn about two P.M. I unsaddled the mules, fed them good. Pam and I went to the cafe to eat. The next morning I told Pam good-bye and headed for the Taylor's place to pickup Pedro. Bob and his wife were home, the boys hadn't got home from school yet. Bob thanked me again for loaning him Pedro. He said he only got to ride him that day from Silsbee. His boys told their friends at school and were going on a ride next Saturday and told some of their friends to go along. Well, this one fellow had two boys and only one horse that he worked a garden with. The boys were the same age as Joe and David, so I let one of his boys ride Pedro.

We all met on this dirt road by the back pasture. The first ride had about six riders. We had the ride every Saturday since, and had more riders each time. Bob told me they had disbanded the ride until next spring. He told me if I got any gentle mules or horses that he could help me sell them. Soon Joe and David got home from school, they were glad to see me. We visited some and I got up and said I needed to catch Pedro and head on the Silsbee. They all said no-no they wanted me to spend the night; I could leave in the morning. I said ok, but I would leave early because they would be busy getting ready for school. We talked till about ten and then went to bed. The next morning I said good-bye and left for the sale barn in Beaumont. I rode hard and got to the sale barn about four P.M. I called my folks and told them I was in Beaumont and would be home in the morning. I put my mules in one pen and Gray Boy in Pedro in another. I went over to the cafe to eat supper. Tom Smith was there so I sat with him and told him I had put my mules in his pens. He said that was fine and I could sleep in his tack and feed room. I told him I was going to make some shutdowns and he might not see me till spring. I got home about ten a.m. the next morning. I called Joe Clark and told him I had his mules and would bring them home in the morning. I lay around the house all evening and told my folks what all I had been doing. I told my mother that her brother would probably be staying in my office building that we were going to work some shutdowns.

The next morning I saddled Gray Boy, put the collars and harness on #2 and #3 mules. I left Pedro at the barn. I then took the mules to Joe's. He was waiting for me when I rode up. I told Joe what all we had done with the mules. They were well broke in to ride, work and pack. I told him his mules were worth at least two hundred and fifty dollars, and if he wanted to sell to let me know. Joe told me he was well pleased with his mules. He paid me for my work and I thanked him, got on Grey Boy and headed for the barn and Pedro. As I rode along I wondered if Uncle Jud would show up to work the shutdowns. Oh well, time will tell.

CHAPTER 5

UNCLE JUD DID SHOW UP AND we worked shutdowns all winter. We worked nearly everyday, sometimes seven days a week. I put all the money I could in the bank so I could meet the note on my ten acres. I did buy another single iron bed and a good sleeping bag and stayed in the cabin with Uncle Jud. He would go back to the farm about every two weeks and buy groceries. He would stay all weekend and come back Sunday evening. If the weather was good I would ride Gray Boy and lead Pedro, they liked to get out and see something different. I made a deal with the bank that they would take the note money out of my account and I wouldn't have to worry with it. By the first of January I had enough money in the bank to pay the note all year. I just kept putting money in, and kept just enough to live on. About the first of February Uncle Jud came back from Newton and told me the fellow that bought the twenty acres of corn was going to want about forty acres of corn if we could supply it. He told him he would check with me, that he would need lots of help. I said yes that I could buy and train mules and horses to work and make money also doing that. Uncle Jud said we could also plant about five acres of sweet potatoes and sell what we didn't want. Jud had bought another set of four-foot mule drawn disks. Also an eight-foot mule drawn fertilize distributor. He looked at it and figured out he could make an eight foot pea planter out of it. Instead of planting one row at a time, we would spread eight feet at a time and disk them in. By the time we made the last shutdown the first part of March we could start planting corn after the 15th. There shouldn't be any frost by then that would hurt anything. The last shutdown ended on a Wednesday, the 10th of March, and all checks would be ready by Friday morning.

We went and got our last check and cashed them. I packed a footlocker with clothes and other things that I might need and let Uncle Jud take it in the truck. I told him I would leave out Monday morning riding Gray Boy and packing Pedro with the army saddle. I would be at the Kirbyville sale barn Wednesday and try to buy mules and horses to make a crop with. Uncle Jud said that would be good, we would sure need more teams and he loaded his pickup and left for Newton. I visited with my folks over the weekend and told them our plans to make a crop of corn, peas and sweet potatoes. Monday morning I saddled Gray Boy and Pedro, I put my bedroll and about 50 lbs. of feed I had left in the feed barrel on Pedro. I got to the General Store in Silsbee about 4 p.m. I put Gray Boy and Pedro in pens back of the store. I then went in the store and visited with the owner, then bought supper and visited some more till closing time. He told me I was welcome to sleep on the back porch like I had before. I told him thanks and would see him in the morning. I then went and fed Pedro and Gray Boy. The next morning I woke up at daylight, fed Gray Boy and Pedro. While the stock was eating the owner had made a pan of biscuits, and then sliced some ham and we had ham and biscuits. I paid him for breakfast and he told me to come back anytime. Then I saddled up and headed for Kirbyville. I made good time and got there about five p.m. I put Grey Boy and Pedro in pens at the sale barn. I then went in and said hi to Pam, she was glad to see me. The next morning I woke up early and fed Pedro and Grey Boy. Pam's red mule (Star) was in a pen close by so I fed him too. While they ate I walked around to see if any mules or horses were there to go through the auction.

When I got back Pam was up and we walked over to the cafe and had breakfast. Afterwards we went back to the sale barn. Pam went inside and started working. I hung around outside. In a little while a man came riding up on a big sorrel part draft horse. I walked over to him and asked if he was for sale and how much he wanted for him. He told me yes he wanted to sell him, that the horse would work and ride; he was about eight years old, about fifteen hands tall and weighed about twelve to thirteen hundred pounds. He wanted to sell the saddle and harness. I asked about the harness and where it was. He told me the collar was all leather (no canvas) and his wife would be there in a little and it was in the truck. I ask how much for all of it. He said he wanted eighty dollars for all of it. I rode the horse a little ways and told him I would buy him. About then his wife drove up, I looked at the harness and paid the man. I ask what the name of the horse and he told me "Big Jim." I told him I could use another good workhorse or mule. He said he might know of one and he would check and see. I told him I would be back next Wednesday. I then put the harness and saddle on the porch with my other tack. I then went to the pens and put Big Jim in the pen with Pedro. I walked around the pens and noticed there were two mules in one of the pens, and a man was standing there looking at them. I ask if they were his mules. He said yes and started telling me how good the mules were, they were both two years old. He had owned them for a year, he had the harness for them, but he had not worked them or rode them. One mule was black with a blue nose, his name is Blackie. The other mule was dark brown with a blue nose, and he called him Brownie.

Both mules were about fourteen hands high. He told me the harness for them was in his truck, and asked if he should put the harness on them to sell the mules with harnesses. I told him that I would want the harness on them so I won't to have to look for it. He asks if I would help bring the harness and put it on them. I told him sure; this would give me a chance to see how the mules acted. The brown mule acted up a little, the black mule just stood still. Tom Smith from the Beaumont sale drove up. I walked over to talk to him. He was glad to see me and wanted me to buy roping calves for him. I told him sure I would buy calves for him, and we went in to get our numbers. Tom said he would go on to the Center, Texas sale barn and be back later that day. I told him to go ahead, I knew the kinds of calves he wanted and I would see him later. When the sale started the mules were set in at thirty dollars each with the harness because the mules were not broke. I bought the mules for seventy dollars for both. When the calves started I bought eight roping calves on Tom Smith's number. I then went to the pens to get the harness off of Brownie and Blackie and took the harness to the porch with the other tack. I moved Brownie and Blackie to a pen by Big Jim and Pedro. Later that day Tom Smith drove up. He only had five calves in his trailer. He was glad when I showed him the eight calves I had bought for him. Tom wanted to pay me for buying calves for him.

I told him no, that he let me stay at his sale barn and I was glad I could do something for him.

Pam worked till she was through and wouldn't have to work Thursday morning. While she worked I fed all of my stock. We walked over to the cafe and ate supper. The next morning we loaded up and headed for Uncle Jud's farm. I put the army saddle on Brownie and loaded all the tack on Brownie. I figured Brownie needed to get use to packing. I put Pedro next to me and tied Brownie to Pedro, I tied Blackie to Brownie, and I tied Big Jim to Blackie. I put the saddle I got with Jim on Blackie. The mules acted up a little with the saddles, but tied between Pedro and Jim they soon learned there was not much they could do. We stopped at Parker's Store in Bleakwood and he was glad to see us. Tom Parker showed us a new horse drawn wagon he had just taken in to sell. The wagon had a steel frame with rubber car tires. The wagon bed was made of Cypress lumber, and it had brakes on all four wheels. It could be pulled with one horse or two. I ask him how much for the wagon and he told me one hundred dollars. I bought the wagon and hitched Big Jim to it. I tied Brownie and Blackie to the back of the wagon. Pam led Pedro and Grey Boy and I drove the wagon. Uncle Jud was surprised to see us coming up the lane with all the stock I had bought. He liked Big Jim and the wagon, and he liked Brownie and Blackie, and was glad I had harness for them. I told my uncle that Jim would work and ride but the mules were only two years old and had not been broke to work or ride. He told me we could put one mule with Big Red and Big Red would teach him to pull a disk. He put the other mule with Big Jim to pull the corn planter.

We got up early the next morning and hooked up the teams like he suggested. Uncle Jud took Big Red and Brownie and hitched them to the disk to make corn rows. I hooked up Blackie to Jim to pull the planter. Brownie didn't like the idea of working but with Big Red there was not much he could do. After about thirty minutes he settled down and started pulling his share. I got in behind Uncle Jud with Blackie and Jim. Blackie started out real good; I had very little trouble with him. We planted corn till about 11 a.m. We took the teams to the barn and let Blackie and Brownie rest till about 2 p.m. We then started planting again. This time Uncle Jud took Rusty and Big Red and disk rows with them. I took Brownie and Jim and planted about two hours. Then I put

Brownie back in the lot and hooked up Blackie with Jim and planted till about 6 p.m. and we stopped for the day. We kept this up till Tuesday about noon. That afternoon Pam and I saddled up Star and Grey Boy and rode to Kirbyville sale barn. We got to the sale barn about four p.m. put mules in separate pens for the night.

The next morning I woke up about daylight, I fed all the stock. In a little while Pam came out and headed for the office to work. About eight thirty the man I bought Big Jim from showed up on a nice gray horse. He saw me and rode over; he was riding bare back with a halter and a half hitch rope on his nose. I told him that was a nice horse and asked if he was for sale. He said yes and he will work and ride. The horse is 3/4 Quarter horse and 1/4 Percheron, and his bloodline goes back to Leo, a well-known Quarter horse. I asked how much he wanted and what his name was. The horse's name is Leo and he would have to have one hundred dollars for him with just the halter and lead rope. I could see the horse was not the average horse and I liked him real well. I put my saddle on him and rode around a little and paid the man. I took Leo and put him with Grey Boy to see how they would be together. Leo was about fifteen hands.

I was standing by the pens looking at Leo thinking how nice he looked and I thought he could be an all around horse and do it well. Just then a truck drove up pulling a red stock trailer with a metal top. The man got out and walked to back of the trailer and stood looking inside. I walked over to see what he had in the trailer. There stood a dapple Grey mule about fourteen hands tall. He had a good head, good neck and withers, everything on the mule looked good till I looked at his pastern and fetlock. His right hind hoof looked like a football. It was all infected and bleeding and oozing bad. I asked what happened to the mules' leg. The man told me he got tangled in barbed wire and he didn't know it for about three days. He took him to the vet, and he gave him a shot for lockjaw and gave him some medicine for it but it hadn't done any good. He had tried everything he knew and anything anyone said, but the mule just keeps going down hill. He has lost probably two hundred pounds. I asked him how long he owned him. He said he bought Jake at six months old. His mother is a Dapple Grey Quarter Horse and the jack is a light Grey about fifty-four inches high.

CHAPTER 6

HE SAID THE MARE HAD BEEN on the racetrack and for a quarter mile was never beat. The owner started hauling her to rodeos, she made a good dogging horse and lots of cowboys wanted to use her for dogging. Then one night he came home from a rodeo, turned her out in a small pasture. The next morning the neighbors jack was out in the pasture with her. The next spring she had this mule colt, and he bought the colt at six months old. He named him Jake and raised him up and kept him gentle, he never offered to kick of bite. Jake was raised with another plow horse he had. They would run and play and Jake turned out to be very fast. When Jake was twenty-two months old, his boys started to ride him a little at a time bareback, one would ride the plow horse and the other would ride Jake. Then he got tangled in the bob wire and he couldn't get him well so he brought him here to get what he could. I told him I would give forty dollars for him if he would deliver him to my uncles farm about sixteen miles away and bring me back here. He said ok, if we could leave now that he lived in Woodville and needed to get home.

I told Pam I was taking Jake to the farm and would be back in about an hour and a half. When we got to the farm my uncle came out to see what I had. When he saw his leg, he said just put him in the lot. While we did that my uncle caught Pedro and put him in the pen with Jake. I told my uncle I would be back in the morning. We got in the truck and headed for Kirbyville. When we got to the sale barn I wrote out a receipt for Jake and he signed it, I paid him cash and he left for Woodville. I went inside and told Pam I as back. She told me the Walker Brothers are looking for me and was probably around the pens. I walked over to the pens and they were there under the big oak trees. They told me they had been to Colorado, and some of the riders from up there watching us and to price Jackson and Koko. I told them at the end of the week we'd auction them off. At the end of the week they had been watching Jackson and Koko and they were ready to buy. They bought Jackson and Koko for seven hundred each. Stafford wouldn't sell Sandy at all and we brought him back. They told me they needed two mules and they would probably sell them in Colorado this fall when they went on another ride.

I told the Walker's all about Brownie and Blackie that they needed a little more riding and if they wanted them now I would sell them tomorrow for three hundred each. They said the price was ok. I ask them what they did for a living. They told me they were partners in the rice farming and they also had about five hundred head of cows and they needed the mules now to work cows on. I drew them a map how to get to the farm. They said they would go home and come back with the trailer and cash tomorrow morning. There weren't any horses or mules at the sale barn that I liked, so I brushed Leo and Grey Boy and Star. Pam worked late and finished all the bookkeeping. We left out early the next morning, Pam rode Star and I rode Grey Boy and led Leo. Just as we went through Newton the Walker's caught up with us. They stayed behind and followed us to the farm. Blackie and Brownie were still in the lot. We tied Star, Leo and Grey Boy. Then we caught the mules. Pam took her saddle and put it on Blackie and I put my saddle on Brownie. Pam and I rode the mules a little, and then offered for the Walker's to ride. They said no, they were satisfied. We took our saddles off and loaded the mules. The Walker's paid me cash, and left for Beaumont. I went over to Uncle Jud and paid him a hundred dollars for helping break the mules. I then paid Pam sixty dollars for her part for riding the mules. Then went to Aunt Willie and gave her forty dollars for cooking and whatever. She was very happy I did that and Uncle Jud was too. After dinner Uncle Jud said we should go see if we can help Jake with his foot. I told my uncle I paid forty dollars for Jake, and that was probably twenty dollars too much. My uncle said no that was forty dollars too much. We went to the lot and Jake was lying down. Uncle Jud said to get a halter and three ropes. I put the halter on Jake, my uncle told me to talk to him in a low voice. While I did this he tied a rope around his neck, then took the other end put it around Jake's good leg then pulled it up toward his neck and tied it to the rope around his two front legs to the left hind leg. This way Jake could not get up. He then told me to get my saddle pad and jacket and put the pad under Jake's head. This would help keep dirt out of his eyes.

While I did this, he took a rope and tied his sore leg to a post so he couldn't kick backwards and took another rope and tied it to a tree so he couldn't kick forwards. He then took a shovel and dug a hole about ten feet from Jake and built a fire in the hole. He had a grill about twenty inches wide and four feet long that he put over the fire. He then went to the house and came back with a three pound coffee can that he kept used grease in. The can was about half full and he put it over the fire. While the grease was getting hot he took a knife and cut away all the proud flesh on Jake's sore. Soon the grease was boiling hot. He told me to put my jacket over Jake's head and try to hold him still, but do not grab his ears. He then took a pair of pliers and got the boiling hot grease and poured it on Jake's sore. Jake brayed and hollered, tried to kick. I kept his head covered and kept talking to him. While this was happening my uncle went to the barn and came back with a can of sulfur. He mixed grease and sulfur till it was a paste. He asked Pam to go to the house and bring back a big long white towel. He cut the towel into four long strips. He then applied the paste to the entire sore with all the paste he could put on it. He then took one of the towel strips and wrapped the leg from the hoof to end of the sore, he took a safety pin and pinned it at the end. Then he took a second peace of towel and wrapped it again and pinned it.

We then untied Jake and took the halter off. My uncle told me to stay with him till he wanted to get up, and keep petting and talking so he doesn't give up. If he is by himself with just Pedro he might give up. If he gives up he will die. I stayed with him for about two hours; I kept talking and petting him till he got up. Jake tried to walk but still wouldn't put his hoof down. He stayed up on his feet, ate some feed and drank some water. Pedro stayed with him anywhere he went in the lot. I got a brush and brushed him and kept talking to him. My uncle told me to get my sleeping bag and my tarp and when Jake lay down he wanted me to lay with him. He didn't want Jake to give up after all we did for him. That evening Jake lay down and I put my bedroll at his shoulder. When Aunt Willie had supper ready my uncle ate first and I stayed with Jake. Then I ate supper and Uncle Jud stayed with Jake. That night I covered Jake with the tarp and I used a little over my bedroll. I slept all night with my hand touching Jake. Every time Jake moved, I would pet him and talk to him. When daylight came Jake and I woke up about the same time. I got up and put my bedroll on the fence and folded the tarp. Jake got up and hobbled over and drank some water. I went and got some feed and fed Pedro and Jake. In a little bit Uncle Jud came out and ask if Jake was alive. I told him yes and he had drunk water and is now eating. He told me that staying all night with him probably gave him the will to live. He then cleaned the wound and put fresh sulfur paste on it every morning for three days. The fourth day Jake didn't limp at all.

We saddled Star and Grey Boy and would go riding, and take Pedro and Jake with us. Soon we would saddle Leo and Jake and ride on short trips. Before long we would lope Leo and Jake three or four hundred yards. At first they would blow pretty hard. Soon they would hardly blow at all. Then we would run for a hundred yards. I would put Pam and Leo on my right and pretend we were racing. Leo could not out run Jake. Jake was always about three feet ahead of Leo. As we were walking Jake and Leo back to the farm I told Pam about the rodeo that was coming up at Jasper. I told her I was going to enter the bareback and saddle bronco riding and was thinking about entering the steer wrestling too, and asked if she would haze for me on Leo, and I would dog off Jake. She told me that she had never done that but she would do her best if I would show her what to do. The next day we were riding on this dirt road. Pam and I would lope along and I would show her how to haze on Leo. We practiced this routine till Tuesday morning. Tuesday afternoon we saddled Star and Grey Boy and Jake. We led Leo with no saddle and headed for Kirbyville sale barn.

We got to the sale barn about four p.m. I put Leo and Jake in one pen and Star and Grey Boy in another pen. Pam went to the office to start on her bookkeeping and I fed everything. In a few minutes T. Porter came walking up. He asked if I was going to the Jasper rodeo next Saturday night. I told him yes, I was going to enter the bareback and saddle bronco riding and was considering the steer wrestling. I laughed and said I have my own dogging team. He asked me where my dogging team is. I laughed and said you're looking at them. The Grey horse is my hazing horse and that dapple mule is my dogging mule. I told Porter the Grey horse goes back to Leo on the sire side and 3/4 Quarter and 1/4 Percheron on the dame side. The mule Jake goes back to a dogging mare of Quarter Blood and a fifty-four inch light Grey Jack. I told him the mule can run as fast as the Grey horse, and that is the same mule with the sore leg he saw in the red trailer a few weeks ago. Porter told me if he is that good he would like to use him in the dogging. I then told him Pam was going to haze for me on Leo.

He said if she was going to haze for me, maybe she could haze for him. I told him we had been practicing what to do and I think she would do fine. Porter told me he had sold his roping horse. This man called him looking for a roping horse for his son and wanted a seasoned horse that knew what to do. He wanted to know if I would sell my roping horse. I told him I guess so, he is sixteen years old and would not be cheap. They came out to my house and I saddled my horse. I always kept two or three roping calves. They roped three calves and asked how much. I priced him fifteen hundred thinking he wouldn't buy him. He pulled out his checkbook and wrote me a check. Now I have to look for a new roping horse. I told Porter that he could try Leo that he could take him home and see. He could try him this evening and work with him till Friday and bring him to Jasper Saturday. Pam would need him to haze on. Porter said ok, he would go home and get his trailer. He lived about three miles from the sale barn on Hwy. 1013. I told Porter I could saddle Grey Boy and lead Leo and be there in twenty-five or thirty minutes. He couldn't go home and get his trailer that quick. Porter said o.k. he would drive his truck and stay ahead of me. When we got there Porter put his calves in the roping chute and asked if I would work the gate. I said o.k. Leo did good, just needed to keep the rope tight. I went back to the sale barn.

Wednesday morning I woke up about daylight, fed my mules and walked around visiting, no horses or mules showed up. Pam worked late and got all the book work done so we could leave early Thursday a.m. for the farm. When we got to Parker's Store we stopped to say hello. Parker told me he had a saddle I might want; we tied out mules and went to see the saddle. I was surprised; he had a rodeo bronco saddle. Parker told me the saddle was almost new, that a fellow traded it for a regular saddle and he would take fifty dollars for it. I bought the saddle and put it on top of Jake's saddle and tied it good and headed for the farm. The next day I rode Jake and Pam rode Star, we gave them a good work out. Saturday morning Pam and I saddled up Star, Grey Boy, Jake and Pedro, and headed for Jasper. I put the bronc saddle on Pedro and also my rodeo duffel bag.

We got to Jasper before noon, rode to the rodeo grounds, tied out stock at the back and went to a cafe to eat. After dinner we went back to the rodeo office. I entered the bareback, saddle bronco riding and the steer dogging. In a little while Porter showed up and entered the calf roping and steer dogging. Then two cowboys drove up and came over. Porter introduced me to them. They were Homer and Norm. They asked us what we were going to do, that the dogging horses they usually use are at a rodeo in Lake Charles. Porter showed them what we were going to use. They looked at Jake and grinned. Don't laugh he told him that mule is fast. I told him I had two openings if they wanted to ride him. They said ok, they would try him too. The calf roping was first and Porter won the roping with eleven seconds flat. The bareback was next and I won second place, I won first place in the saddle bronco riding. In the steer dogging Porter won with eight seconds flat. The fellow with his own team won second. Norm won third on Jake, and I won fourth on Jake and Homer's steer dog fell and didn't win any money, but Jake did well on all runs.

After the rodeo we all got out paychecks and paid Pam for hazing. Then Porter came over to talk about Leo and how much it would take to buy him. I told him if I kept Leo I would probably make five to eight hundred with him this summer at rodeos. He thought so too, and he thought Leo could be just as good with proper training. He told me he would pay twelve hundred for Leo if I would take it. I told him that was the same amount I was thinking and he could have him. He told me o.k. and wrote me a check. Then he asked me if I was going to the rodeo in Dequincy, La. next Saturday. I said yes and probably Deridder the following weekend. I was going home for a few days and would call Clyde to see if he was going and hitch a ride with him. He had a stock trailer and plenty of room for Jake and me. Clyde will probably be a pickup man and bring his horse "Chico." It was about ten-thirty p.m. Pam when I saddled up and headed for Newton. It was a full moon and I got to the farm about one a.m. The next morning my folks drove up and had dinner. I ask them to take some things home for me. I got my footlocker and put all my checks in it along with some of my clothes and my rodeo stuff and bronc saddle. I would be home probably Friday, and go to a rodeo Saturday at Dequincy. My folks left after dinner, I told them thanks for taking my stuff.

Pam and I saddled up Tuesday afternoon and rode to Kirbyville. Wednesday morning about nine a man drove up with a trailer. He unloaded a nice bay horse about fifty-four inches high. I walked over and I ask him about the horse, and he told me he was very gentle, the only thing he won't do is run. He has a good running walk, and he will trot and lope. He needed a horse that he can catch cows on. He said his name was Chunky, and he didn't care about catching anything. He said he works cows for a lot of people and needs a better horse. I asked how much for the horse and saddle and he said one hundred dollars. I paid him for Chunky and he got in his truck and left. I took Chunky over to the big oak trees and tied him to the pipe fence. I walked around looked at stock in the pens, nothing interesting to me so I went back to Chunky and was brushing and talking to him. I rode him a little; he did have a good running walk. Late that evening the Taylor's came driving up, saw me and drove over to where I was. He told me they were starting the Saturday morning ride, they might have about fifteen or twenty riders. They wanted to know if I had any gentle horses or mules. I showed them Chunky and untied him and told David to get on and ride. He rode a little ways and came back grinning. Chunky was not quite as tall as the roan horse of Joe's. Bob ask how much for the horse and saddle. I told him one hundred twenty five dollars. David spoke up and said he wanted Chunky and he would sell Dan and his saddle. I told Bob I was headed by his house in the morning, but he said he would be working tomorrow and no one would be home. I told him that was ok; I would put Chunky in the lot and put the saddle and tack in his barn. I gave him my new address and phone number, and told him he could mail me a check when he sold whichever horse he wanted. That way he would not be out any money. Also horses were going up in price. Dan and saddle should bring a hundred fifty to a hundred seventy-five dollars. Bob liked the part about not being out any money. They were all happy and left for home.

The next morning I told Pam good-bye, I would see her in about a week in between rodeos. I got to the Taylor's and left Chunky like I said I would. I spent the night in Silsbee at the General Store like I usually did and I put Grey Boy, Jake, and Pedro in separate pens. The next morning I headed for the Beaumont sale yard and got there about four p.m. Tom was outside and came over to talk. There was a nice horse trailer parked there with a for sale sign on it. Tom told me it was four foot by ten foot. A fellow left it here to sell and said he needed a bigger trailer. It had a large saddle storage area, a spare tire and a two-stack saddle rack. The horse side was thirty inches wide and about eighteen inches to walk in with a horse. It had an escape door where you put saddles and feed. I asked how much for the trailer. Tom told me the owner wanted three hundred dollars for it. I told him I would keep it in mind.

Then Norm came over, the fellow that was at the Jasper rodeo. I liked him when we met in Jasper; he helped me with my bronco riding and told me things to watch for. He also helped me set my bronco saddle and bareback rigging. He asked if I was going to the Dequincy rodeo. I said yes, that I was going to call Clyde when I got home and see about going with him. Norm said he knew Clyde also and maybe he had room for one more. I said lets find out right now and I tied my stock and we went in and called him. Clyde was home and I told him about our plans and asked if he had room for us. Clyde said sure, that he would pick up me and my mule up about two p.m. and pick up Norm at the sale barn next and we would all go to De Quincy together. I said good-bye to Norm and would see him tomorrow. I got home about six p.m., put my mules in the pasture and went in and visited with my folks. I told them I had to go to the bank in the morning and dad said he would take me. I took my footlocker and rodeo stuff to my cabin. Dad had already put my bronco saddle in the barn. I ate supper with my folks and then went to the barn and fed.

The next morning I made out my bank deposit. I showed them the check for Leo and they couldn't believe a horse would bring that much. Then I told them he would make more than that with Leo this summer, and I told them all about Jake and what all uncle Jud done to get him well, and how much I made on him at the Jasper rodeo. Then I said lets go to the bank, that Clyde was going to pick us up after dinner and we were going to De Quincy and would not be back till maybe two a.m.

We got the bank just as they opened and I made my deposit. I noticed just as we got to the bank there was a 1946 Ford panel truck with a for sale sign on it. I asked the bank man about the truck and he told me they had financed for a man and he got caught with D.W.I. and couldn't drive for a year. I asked what the pay off was and he said the pay off was nine hundred dollars. I told him I wanted to drive it and he said o.k., that it had less than eight thousand miles on it. My dad rode with me and the truck sounded good. I told the bank man I would take it and I wrote the bank a check for the truck. I told dad he could go home, that I had to go to the feed store, and would be there in a little while.

I got home and put the feed in the barn. I fed my stock and got four empty gallon paint cans that I got working shut downs. I filled two cans with feed to take to the rodeo. I got all my rodeo stuff ready, ate dinner and saddled Jake. Clyde drove up in a little while and I loaded Jake and all my rodeo stuff in the back of Clyde's truck. I asked dad if he would feed for me and of course he said yes. We headed for the sale barn to pick up Norm. I told Clyde to stop at a gas station and I would fill his truck up. He said he was going to De Quincy any way. I said it is your truck and your trailer and I could gas up his truck. After getting gas we picked up Norm and were on our way. Tom Smith was there and I told him I wanted the trailer. I would be there about 9 a.m. Sunday if that were ok, Tom said fine, and that he would tell the owner to be here. As we rode along Norm said he could help me with any bareback rigging if I wanted and I said I would appreciate any help he could give. When we got to De Quincy we went on out to the rodeo grounds and Norm said to get my rigging and he would show me what I could do to improve it. He looked at the rigging, then said lets go over to the store across the street.

Clyde unloaded our stock and tied them to the truck. Norm started picking out things we would need. He got a hand crank drill, a set of drill bits, a pair of needle nose pliers, a roll of duct tape, and a pair soft leather gloves. I paid for everything and we went back to the truck. First he unlaced the little end of the handhold. Then he made the handle hump up by pushing it forward. I marked the three holes through the rigging, then drilled 3/8 holes and re-laced the handle. Then he took a six-inch piece of 1/4-inch rope and laid it long ways on the handle. Then he told me to put my hand in the handle to see if it fit better. I tried my hand and it did fit better. Then Norm took about an 18-inch piece of duct tape and folded it long ways with sticky part out. Then he wrapped the rigging handle with the tape and he told me to get a glove that I would ride with and put it on, and put my hand in the handle. I did this and grabbed a good hold. I could hardly get my hand out. Norm said this would help a lot when riding big stout horses. Norm was a little older and I knew he had given me good advice. I thanked him and put my rigging in my rodeo bag. Then we went to the rodeo office and entered in the same events as usual.

In a little while Porter drove up. He was pulling a two-horse trailer and he had his thirteen-year-old son, Mike, with him. I asked where the rest of his family was and he said his ten-year-old son, Jeff, had a little league baseball game and couldn't make it. He had brought Mike's horse and Leo in the trailer. He parked his truck by us, then went to the office to enter the calf roping and dogging. In a little while Porter came back and Homer was with him. Homer asked if Jake was available for him to dog off on. I said yes I had saved a ride for him. While we were talking a man walked up leading a sorrel horse. He wanted to see if his horse could run and wanted to have a race. I asked how far and he said a hundred yards or so. I told him I would run Jake with his horse that I wanted to see if my mule could run too. I asked how much he wanted to bet and he said how about a hundred dollars. I told him that was o.k. with me. There was a straight dirt road close by so he and I stepped off about a hundred yards and I took a stick and marked a line across the road. I asked who was going to ride his horse. He said his son would ride. I looked at his son and saw that he was about a hundred and fifty pounds. Porter told me Mike had ridden in some races and asked if we could put Mike's saddle on Jake. I told the man that would be fine, that Mike could ride my mule.

We each put up a hundred dollars and let Clyde hold the money. Porter and the man went to the finish line and they wanted to know if I was going. I said no I wanted to see that they started o.k. I called it - on your mark-get set-go they jumped off to a good start and I hollered at Jake and he took off and jumped ahead and crossed the line about fifteen feet ahead of the sorrel horse. I collected my money and gave Mike ten dollars for winning the race. He was real happy and said to let him know if I had another race. The rodeo would start soon and

Mike wanted to ride Jake in the grand entry. I said ok, and I rode his horse. When the rodeo was over Porter won second in the calf roping and first in the dogging. I won first in the bareback riding and second in the saddle bronco riding. Norm won first in saddle bronco riding and second in the bareback riding. Norm won second in the dogging and I won third in the dogging. I had won altogether two hundred and twenty five dollars plus ninety dollars on the race. Clyde did well; he was pickup man on Chico and made money hazing in the dogging.

We got to the Beaumont sale barn about 1:30 a.m., we let Norm out and we all said good-bye. There was an all night gas station open and I had Clyde stop and fill up his truck. We got to my place about two a.m. I unloaded Jake and got my rodeo stuff and we said our good-byes. The next morning I ate breakfast with my folks and I told them I was going to look at a trailer to haul Jake with. I left about eight-thirty and got there early so I could look the trailer over good. It had a place to lock the tailgate when it is closed and also to lock the escape door. In a little while, Tom and another man came up. He said he would take three hundred for the trailer I said o.k. and wrote him a check. When I got home I took the wheels off and checked the bearings to see if they had plenty of grease and they were packed real well. I then went to town to the lumberyard. I bought a box of eight pad locks all keyed alike. I would need two locks on the trailer and one for the feed room in the barn and one on my footlocker. Norm had told me that at big rodeos you need to lock your stall door or someone will take your horse stall. Then I bought a 4 by 8 by 3/4 plywood and had them cut it two foot by eight foot. Then I had him cut it six foot six inches. Then I bought a 2 by 6 by 8 foot board and had him cut it in twenty-two inch pieces. I also bought a piece of 4" thick foam two foot by eight foot to sleep on. I loaded all this stuff and paid him. Then I went to a carpet store and bought a remnant piece of carpet five by eight and took everything home. When I got home I had a letter from the Taylor's, it was a check for one hundred and twenty five dollars. I went back to town and put it in the bank along with seventy-five dollars cash. I went back home and started working on my truck. First I put the carpet in and cut around the fender wells. Then I got four- one gallon buckets that I got at the shutdowns. I filled the buckets with dirt and put the lids on. Then I put two buckets in front of the fender well on the right side, and two buckets in back of the fender on the carpet. Then I put a 2 by 6 by 22" on top of the buckets and laid the plywood six foot six inched on top of the 2 by 6's.

Then I anchored the plywood to the side of the truck with wire so it would not slide off. Then I put the four-inch foam on the plywood and cut it the same length as the plywood. I would use the piece for a pillow. Dad walked up about this time, and helped me put my footlocker in the truck. I told him I would be sleeping in the truck at rodeos. I would be going to De Ridder for a Friday and Saturday night rodeo this weekend and would be back here Sunday. Then in two weeks I would be at Alexandria for a three-day rodeo, and I would be home that Sunday. Tuesday morning I loaded Jake in the trailer, put my bronco saddle and Jake's saddle in the saddle compartment along with my rodeo bag and a five-gallon bucket of feed. I got to the Kirbyville sale barn that morning and stopped and showed Porter my truck and trailer. He liked everything and said he would be at De Ridder Friday morning. I told him I would save him a place to park next to me. Porter already had his camper loaded on his truck. He said his wife and Jeff would be there Saturday morning. I said why don't you bring Jeff's horse to ride in the Grand entry and Mike can ride Jake. Porter said ok, that Jeff likes to be included too and he thanked me.

Then I showed Porter the locks on my trailer. He said his trailer has a place to lock the doors and said he should start locking his. I reached in the truck and got a lock and two keys and gave him a lock. I told him I had bought eight locks all keyed alike, if we go to Alexandria we could lock our stalls. Porter said that was a good idea. I told him I was headed to the farm in Newton and would probably bring Pam in my truck early Wednesday. He said that would be fine. I went on to the farm and I turned Jake loose with Star. Uncle Jud was in the cornfield pulling corn so I went out helped load corn. Then Pam and Aunt Willie started canning corn. We hauled the next load and put it in barn for feed. We worked Big Red and Rusty with the big wagon till noon. After dinner we worked Big Jim with the one horse rubber-tired wagon. We put the first load on the front porch and the next load in the barn. Then Uncle Jud and I shucked corn the rest of the evening. The next morning I took Pam to the sale barn in the truck. I stayed and helped around the sale all day. Pam worked late and we went to the farm that night.

Thursday evening I left for De Ridder, I found a good place to park for Porter and me. I staked Jake and let him eat grass. That night I tried my bed out and slept real well. The next morning cowboys started coming from everywhere. I took a rope and tied it to a tree and to my truck so Porter would have a place to park. Porter and his son Mike got here after dinner. He said Jeff had another ball game and would be here Saturday morning and would all sleep in his camper on his truck. We went to the rodeo office and entered the usual events. Homer and Norm drove up, they also entered the usual events. Homer and Norm both wanted to use Jake in the dogging. I said fine. Clyde couldn't be here and Porter was going to haze on Leo. Mike wanted to ride Jake in the Grand Entry. I said sure, that I would ride Jeff's horse. Mike wanted to know if he could ride Jake around some. I said ok, and put Jake's saddle on him and adjusted the stirrups to fit him. I told him not to tell anyone how fast Jake was. If someone wants to race don't say anything, just come tell me and I will handle it. When the rodeo started there were twenty bareback riders so I only got one horse. The horse didn't buck well and I didn't make any money. In the saddle bronc I won second and Norm won first the first night. The second night I won third and Norm won fourth. In the dogging the first night I won first, Homer won second, Porter won third and Norm won fourth. The next night a fellow named Ike won first in the dogging, and Porter hazed for him then Norm won second, Homer won third, and Porter won fourth. I didn't place.

The next morning I headed for the farm in Newton. I visited a while and I told Uncle Jud I had to go home and would be back Tuesday to help with the corn. I got home about eleven and ate dinner with my folks. Jake was glad to be with Gray Boy and Pedro. Monday morning I went to the bank to make a deposit, I had done pretty well at the rodeo. I went by the feed store and bought some feed. I told my folks I would leave for Newton in the morning. I would help with the corn and maybe sweet potatoes and I would bring some back. I would take Gray Boy with me to ride into Kirbyville on Tuesday. I would try to buy mules or horses to sell. I would go back to Newton and stay till Monday morning because there was a three-day rodeo Thursday, Friday, and Saturday. I would be back home Sunday evening and Dad told me he would feed for me.

Next morning I loaded Gray Boy in the trailer and went to Newton. I helped my Uncle Jud gather corn and put it in the barn for feed. Uncle Jud told me the man that wanted the forty acres of corn came by. When he saw Big Jim pulling the rubber-tired wagon he asked if he could rent the horse and wagon to haul corn. I told him it was ok with me. Whatever he got would be his since he had been taking care of him. Pam and I rode our mules to Kirbyville Sale Barn Tuesday. I looked for horses and mules but nothing showed up. I helped with the crops and went home Monday morning with about three bushels of sweet potatoes. I turned Gray Boy out with Jake and Pedro. The next morning I trimmed Jake's feet and cut his mane. Wednesday morning I loaded Jake in the trailer and put my rodeo stuff in the front part of the trailer. I told my folks I would be back Sunday evening or Monday. I drove to the sale barn in Kirbyville and stopped to check with Porter. He said he would leave Thursday morning, that Mike would be with him and Jeff and his wife would be there over Saturday. He said Jeff had another ball game Friday night. I told him I would hold a space for him to park and lock two stalls for his two horses.

I then left for Alexandria. I stopped at Parker's Store and visited with Tom and I bought some groceries in case there was not any cafe's close by in Alexandria. I bought a jar of peanut butter, a pint of May haw jelly that Mrs. Parker had made. I bought some tablespoons, forks, and knives to use to make sandwiches, and two packages of hamburger buns. Also three tin coffee cups, and one gallon of orange juice. I had brought and old ice box about 16 by 16 by 24" long and I put the orange juice in the icebox with some ice to keep it cool. I got to Alexandria about one p.m. and I picked a good place to park under some big oak trees. The first thing I did was lock up three stalls close by. I unloaded Jake and let him eat some grass, then I put him in a stall for the night and gave him some hay and feed. The next morning Porter and his son Mike drove up around eleven and parked next to me. We went to the rodeo office and entered our usual events. There were fifteen doggers, so we had ten doggers during the rodeo and the next morning we had a catch-up in the dogging, we had to catch up to complete a go around. Jake was busy at night during the rodeo and next morning doing a catch up. This went on all three days.

Friday evening Mrs. Porter and Jeff drove up about five and said the ball game had been rained out. Mrs. Porter and Jeff had not eaten supper, thinking they could eat at the concession stand but it was closed. They did not have permit and it would be Saturday before they could get one. Jeff was hungry and wanted to know what they were going to do. I spoke up and said how about a peanut butter and jelly sandwich and orange juice. Jeff said that would be great and Mike said he could go for that so I went to the truck and got all the stuff I had bought at Parker's store. Mrs. Parker started making sandwiches while I got the cups and started pouring orange juice. We all had orange juice and peanut butter and jelly sandwiches.

Saturday about two p.m. a fellow came riding up on a bay horse. He looked like he might weight about hundred and sixty pounds and he was looking for someone to have a horse race with. I told him I might run my mule against his horse and asked how much he wanted to bet. He said he would like to bet a hundred dollars so I told him if he would put up a hundred and ten dollars, I would put up a hundred. He had a good horse and I needed a little odds. Also his horse would have to beat by four feet, and for a hundred yards. He said that was ok with him, and asked who was going to ride my mule and I told him Mike would ride him. Porter wanted to bet twenty dollars also and the fellow said ok.

Mrs. Porter's eyes got big, and she said are you going to bet on the mule? Porter said yes, he liked to take chances. We stepped off about a hundred yards. Porter got on the finish line and I went to the starting line. I called it on your mark-get set- go. Jake leaped out in front and crossed the finish line ten feet ahead of the bay horse. I collected my money and gave Mike ten dollars. He was happy again. Mrs. Porter couldn't believe a mule could run that fast. Then Porter told his wife about the race at De Ridder last weekend and that was how Mike made ten dollars in a race. I didn't make money on every bronc I got on, but over three days I did make money in all three events. I had eight different cowboys dogging on Jake, by the end of the rodeo all of them had placed in the dogging. Sunday I left for the farm in Newton. After dinner I left for home, I had made a little over four hundred dollars at the Alexandria rodeo. I put two hundred dollars in the bank. Jake and I went to rodeos all over Louisiana, some in Mississippi, and some in East Texas. Jake had made a good name as a dogging mount. Rodeo season was slowing down some. One day I was at the sale barn in

Kirbyville talking to Porter and he wanted to know if I was going to the state fair and rodeo in Texarkana. I told him it was a pretty good size rodeo for me so the competition would be great. I asked if he thought I could make any money, that it was a ten-day rodeo. Porter told me he was thinking about going. He thought I would have lots of cowboys wanting to use Jake in the dogging, and he thought I could make money in the bronc riding events too. The rodeo would start on a Thursday and be on for ten days with two rodeos on Saturday. If I would go he would go for sure. I told him ok, I would go. I would go on Tuesday and find us a good place to park and lock two stalls for Jake and Leo.

I went back home and told my folks I was going to Texarkana to a rodeo. I would be gone about two weeks. Dad told me he would feed Gray Boy and Pedro for me so I started loading my rodeo stuff Saturday. I had bought two thirty-gallon trash cans and I filled them with feed plus one five-gallon bucket. I put two empty one gallon buckets in the trailer and also two bales of hay. Uncle Jud had told me that I could put sand in a gallon bucket and pour diesel fuel in it and it would burn for hours, and when I wanted to put the fire out just put the lid on it. I put my wood icebox in the truck and I put two gallons of orange juice and two jars of peanut butter and two jars of jelly in the icebox.

Monday morning I loaded Jake and headed for Newton. I stopped at the Kirbyville sale barn and told Porter I was going to Texarkana, that I would stay tonight at the farm and leave for Texarkana Tuesday morning. I stopped at Parker's Store and bought two gallons of diesel fuel in case I wanted a fire to sit around. I spent the night at Uncle Jud's farm and I left out early for the long trip. I told them I would be back a week from Sunday. Six hours later I got to Texarkana and picked a good place to set up camp. Then I went and locked two stalls for Leo and Jake. I unloaded Jake and let him eat some grass and I put a block of hay out also so he could take his choice to eat. In a little while a fellow drove up in a panel truck. I walked over to talk to him and he told me he was a horse shoer, and he traveled to rodeos to shoe horses. I asked him if he would trim Jake's feet and see if I had been trimming right. He said sure, so I went over and got Jake and he trimmed him up and gave me a few pointers on trimming hoofs. I took Jake back to the trailer and let him eat hay. Then I took a rope and tied it to a tree and to my truck so Porter could park next to me. Then I went to the rodeo office and entered in the bareback and saddle bronc ridding, also in the steer wrestling. I told them Porter would be here tomorrow to enter the dogging and calf roping. They said they would go ahead and put his name down. Homer and Norm walked up; they were the pick up men for the rodeo. They wanted me to save a place for them to use Jake in the dogging and I said ok. It turned out there was twenty cowboys entered in the dogging. I booked eight of them on Jake. We all got five steers for the rodeo. All the doggers made money on Jake. I placed in three of the five go round. In the bareback there were fifty riders so we only got two head. I only placed fourth in one go around. In the saddle bronc we got five head and I placed on three. All together I made over nine hundred dollars. Porter did well, too; he hazed on Leo and roped calves also. Leo had made Porter all the money he paid for him the first summer. The bucket of sand with diesel poured on it worked out good. Every morning I would light it and we all gathered around it till it warmed up. The orange juice and peanut butter and jelly saved me a lot of money too.

Sunday morning I loaded up Jake and Porter loaded Leo and we headed for home. I followed Porter to Jasper, he went onto Kirbyville and I turned and went to Newton. I spent the night at the farm and let Jake run with the mules. Tuesday morning I headed for home. ***While driving along I was thinking, I had made enough money to last all winter. I didn't have to work any shutdowns unless I wanted to. I might just do some horse and mule trading. My uncle had told me the fellow who wanted the corn would want another forty acres of it. I thought to myself, he sure does feed a lot of corn. Oh well, time will tell.

CHAPTER 7
May, 1948

Sunday morning, we all met at the big tent. We had church and Ed Brown preached a short sermon. Afterwards, he asked us all about doing this about once a year. He said if we had any suggestions, to write them down and put them in a box on the table. After breakfast, Ed came over and thanked us all for helping. Then we all got started getting ready to go home. I told Porter I would get Cody Tuesday. He thanked me again for letting him use Cody. All Dad had to do was put his bed in the back of the '47 pickup. I had sold the rig he brought. We all got home about noon. Monday morning, I called Big T Trailers in Mesquite. I could see where a small trailer would be handy for hauling corn to be milled. He told me he had a 5' x 12' horse trailer. Most everyone sleeps in their trailers and a 14-foot trailer gives them more room. He told me it has surge brakes and a sliding gate on the back and tandem wheels. It has an escape door on the front. I asked him, what color and how much. He said he could paint it any color and would take $450 for the trailer. Also, he would deliver it with another trailer to Jasper next Tuesday. I told him I would take the trailer and to paint it tan, the same tan he painted my rodeo trailer. I told him I would give the delivery man a check and asked what time he would be in Jasper. He said he should be there about noon, Tuesday week. Tuesday morning, Pam and I loaded the two red donkeys that Tom Smith used on the cattle drive. We stopped by Porters and I told him we were taking the two donkeys to Uncle Jud's. We would come back by after dinner and get Cody and take him to Kirbyville. We would work the sale and take Cody to Nederland Thursday. He thanked me again for Cody.

We worked the sale Wednesday. The only thing I bought was a

box of tack. It had halters, brass D-rings, and some 1/2" cotton rope I could see. I set the price at $5.00. No one else would bid, so I bought it and put my number on it. When we got home, we checked the box. It had two good halters, two leather-covered stirrups, a pair of spurs, two 1/2" ropes with brass snaps, and some brass D-rings. We worked some more on the new tack and feed room. I built some more saddle stands. Harry worked on the 4' x 8' wagon and a couple of two-wheel carts. I asked him about making the carts one foot longer at the front. I wanted to put a 12" x 12" x 3' storage box at the front of the foot space. Harry thought a storage box would be handy, so he added a foot to both two wheel carts. Monday morning, I told Dad we were going to Jasper and told him about the trailer. Then we would go to Uncle Jud's and spend the night, then go to Kirbyville and work the sale, and be back here Thursday. When we got back Thursday, Dad came over and looked at the 5' x 12' trailer. I told him I got this trailer for the same price as the 3' x 8'. We would probably use it to haul corn to the gristmill to grind up for feed. When Harry and Arlene came out, they couldn't believe I got the trailer for $450. Tuesday morning, we went to Uncle Jud's. Pam wanted to ride in the woods back of Uncle Jud's. We were sitting on the front porch talking when T.J. Adams and his wife came driving up. Uncle Jud hollered for them to get out, and I went and got two chairs. We sat there and talked a little, and then T.J. said he was in trouble. He realized he was not going to be able to take the corn crop as he planned. He had said it was for feed but it was actually for a still he had down on the creek. The Sheriff caught him and fined him $5,000. He either had to pay it or go to jail. He wanted to know if Uncle Jud would buy the hundred-acre tract next to him. It was a tract he bought from his brother and it had a separate title. It had a barn, all the timber and minerals. Uncle Jud looked at me and I nodded my head. He then told T.J. he couldn't buy it since he had all he could handle, and asked if he would sell me the land. He said, yes, that he wanted someone who was kind of in the family. He would be glad for me to buy it. I asked about the barn, the contents, how much he wanted for it and if he had a clear title. T.J. said he needed $7,500 for the land and contents. He had to pay the fine and he needed some to live on, and that it did have a clear title. There is a big, gray donkey that he would let him go with the land. I asked him how old the donkey was and he said he was about sixteen, that he bought him when he was one-year old. He also said he would work and ride.

T.J. said about fifty acres are open and the back half is woods with a creek and two or three springs on it. This will leave him with 150 acres. I said let's go to the courthouse and transfer the title to me, that I would pay for the paperwork. I told him if he ever wanted to sell the rest of the land, I would like to buy it and he could live on it the rest of his life. T.J. said he would keep it in mind. Pam and I followed T.J. to the courthouse. The deed was transferred to the Circle W Enterprise and I wrote T.J. a check for the land. I asked T.J. if we could come over and get the donkey and saddle and tack, that I was sure it needed oiling. T.J. said, sure and he said Pete, the donkey's name, probably needed his feet trimmed. We went back to Uncle Jud's and Pam saddled Star, her mule. I saddled one of the red donkeys and put a halter and lead rope on the other. I put a couple of toe sacks on the back of my saddle. We rode up the dirt lane between the corn and sweet potatoes, opened the gate and rode over to the barn. When we got there, Pete, the donkey, was already there. His feet looked bad, they really needed trimming, and he could stand some feeding. I put the old saddle on the other red donkey. There was an old doctor's buggy in the barn. T.J. said the buggy went, too. I told him I would leave it for now. We put all of the leather things in the two toe sacks, tied the sacks to the saddle, and tied Pete to the saddle. We got to Uncle Jud's and he came out to look at Pete. He showed me what to do on Pete's hooves. First, he said, put all the stock in the lot and feed them. Pete was glad to get some feed. Pam and I washed all the collars and harness and saddle. Everything was covered with dirt and dust. When the stock got through eating, I haltered Pete and brought him out of the lot and started brushing him. Pam started oiling the saddle and tack. Uncle Jud told me I could only trim about once a week. If I cut too much I would cripple him. Uncle Jud told me it would take about a month to get his hooves trimmed to normal. Tuesday evening, we drove to the Kirbyville sale barn. I tagged a few cows that came in early. We spent the night at the sale barn in Pam's cabin. After the sale Wednesday, Pam and I went back to Uncle Jud's. Thursday I spent some time with Pete, brushing and feeding him. We also put more oil in the leather things. Friday morning, Pam and I saddled the red donkeys and rode over to the Adam's place. We both liked our investment. Friday evening, we went home to Nederland and I told my folks about the Circle W Enterprise. Friday night, Pam and I were talking; we did not have a dogging team or a good barrel horse. We decided to call the Starr Ranch and see what they had for sale. I knew not to call till Sunday morning as they would be busy with their guests. We told Harry and Arlene and my folks about buying some more horses.

Sunday morning, I called Bill Starr. He was glad to hear from me. He told me they had plenty of horses and the black mules and the red mules were ready, that we could leave about noon and spend the night. All of the guests would be gone and we could pick out the horses that evening and leave out Monday morning early. I told him that sounded good to Pam and me. Pam had never been to that part of Texas, so she was happy we were going. We ate dinner early and told my folks and Harry and Arlene we should be back around noon Monday. When we got to Livingston, we stopped at the same saddle shop. I put a note on his door that we would be back about 9 or 10 a.m. Monday and that I could use some good, used saddles. Then we drove on to the Starr Ranch. I introduced Pam to everyone, and she was surprised at the whole ranch layout. We first looked at the mules. They were real nice. Bill said he had to increase the price on the mules and horses. I told him I understood that the price of everything had gone up. He had to have two hundred a head for the mules and one hundred-fifty a head on the horses. I told Bill I didn't mind paying for good horses and mules. We first looked at the two black mules (for the Walker brothers). Then we looked at the two red mules (for Walker's neighbors). Then we looked at a sorrel horse about 54 inches high, with white mane and tail. They named him Sandy. They had dogged a few steers on him. He was half-Welsh and half-Quarter horse and very fast. Then he showed me a gray horse, half-Welsh, and half-Quarter horse; he had been dogged on some; 54 inches high. I put these two horses in a pen by themselves. I would haul these two in my trailer. Pam saw two sorrel horses, both about 15 hands tall, and she learned their names were Dusty and Snip. Pam wanted a couple of horses to train for barrel racing. Bill said they were fast and should do the job just fine. This made six head, so far. Then Matt showed me two good ranch horses. They were about 15 hands high. Both were sorrel horses with 1/8 Belgian, 1/2 Welsh and the rest

Quarter horse. Very gentle to ride, but had not been worked. This made eight, so far. Then Matt showed us some horses in a lot. They were all sorrels about 53 to 54 inches tall. There were about six or seven in the pen. They were all gentle, broke to ride and work to a two-wheel cart. We picked out three head. This would be eleven head and would be a full load. Then Bill showed me a big donkey, about the same height as Pedro. He was Buckskin in color, dark, with a brown stripe down his back, and shoulder stripe. He was broke to ride and work and was kid gentle. I asked Bill how much, and he said fifty dollars for just the donkey, no saddle, no harness. I told Bill I had a good load picked out but if I can get him in my trailer with the two dogging horses, I would take him. We all went over to the kitchen and ate supper. Then we visited till about nine p.m. Pam and I slept in the panel truck.

Next morning, we loaded up. I put the donkey in the front of the trailer and put the gate between the donkey and the two dogging horses. Matt loaded the rest of the horses in the big trailer. I told Matt I wanted to stop at the saddle shop in Livingston. We left out about 7 a.m. and got to Livingston about 9:30. The owner had found the note I had left. He had five saddles he thought I would like. Two were roping saddles with bull hide covered trees, and three were good riding saddles. The two roping saddles were $75, the three riding saddles were $40 each, and all had saddle pads. I paid him for the saddles and headed for Nederland. We got home about 12:30 p.m. Dad saw us turn off the highway and opened the gates. We unloaded the stock and Matt headed back home. I called the Walker ranch about the mules. They were waiting for my call. They said they would bring the neighbor, they want the red mules. I told them, okay and to turn in at the big, double gates and back up to the barn. I put the buckskin donkey in the lot with Pedro and Gray Boy. We got the mules out and brushed them, and then we saddled them and rode around a little. The Walkers and their friends drove up a little later. They rode the mules and asked how much. I told him $450 each. They each wrote me a check and said they were happy to get good mules. They said they would probably take the mules to Colorado in September.

Dad wanted to know what was I going to do with the donkey. I told him I got a gray donkey with the Adam's land I bought and they would make a good pair to farm with. I told him about the three ponies we had bought and told him to pick out one to pull the new cart. Then we all walked around and looked at the horses. I told Dad what plans I had for the horses. I called Porter and told him about the gray horse, 54 inches high. I needed to train him some more. Porter said he wanted him, he said he would make him a dogging team, using Smokey to haze on. I told him, ok. Harry and Arlene came out when they got off work. They liked all of the horses, especially Buck, the donkey. I told Harry I had already sold four mules, a pair of red mules and a pair of black mules.

Tuesday morning, Pam and I went to Uncle Jud's and I told him about Buck. He said Buck and Pete would make a good pair to farm with. I told him I would bring Buck to Newton, probably next Tuesday. Pam and I drove the '47 pickup to the sale barn. On the way Pam suggested that we bring Gray Boy, my saddle mule, to Newton. That way every Tuesday we could ride our gaited mules to Kirbyville for the sale, then ride back on Thursday to Uncle Jud's, leave Gray Boy and Star at Uncle Jud's and drive back home. I thought that was a good idea, we had plenty of horses in Nederland to ride. We worked the sale barn Wednesday. Porter wanted to know more about the 54" gray horse. I told him, he was from the same ranch as Shorty and Smokey, he was just as fast, and he should make a good dogging horse. Porter told me it didn't look like he was going to find Leo and he wanted to go ahead and buy Smokey and this gray 54" horse. He and Mike could finish training him and asked how much I wanted for both horses. I told him, two thousand for both horses. He said that each horse is worth that. I told Porter I knew the horses were worth more, but I was in a position that I could help him. He was always helping me and I wanted to help him. Porter asked about bringing the gray dogging horse and my dogging team to his place Saturday morning and we could use his four steers to try them on. We said, ok, we would be there about 9 a.m. I would put all three in my stock trailer. I told Pam we could bring Grey Boy to Newton later. We worked the sale barn and spent the night at Uncle Jud's Wednesday, and went home Thursday.

Friday night, Harry and Arlene came out and spent the night. I asked if they wanted to go to Porter's place in Kirbyville, that I had the gray horse sold and Porter had steers to train on. We could come back Saturday. They both said, yes. Saturday, we loaded the horses in the 14-foot stock trailer. We got to Porter's about 9 a.m. Porter had the steers in the pen. We saddled the horses. I put a saddle I bought in Livingston on the gray horse; it had a low cantle and would make a good dogging saddle. Porter was glad I brought the saddle since he didn't have a good dogging saddle. Porter asked how much for the dogging saddle. I told him, nothing, he could have the saddle with the horse. Porter just smiled and added $100 to the amount and handed me a check. First, Porter dogged a steer, and Mike hazed on Smokey. Then Mike dogged on Sandy and Jeff hazed on Smokey. Then I dogged a steer on Sandy and Pam hazed. Every horse worked well. Porter was happy with his team. This way he and Mike would have a team to use when I was out of town at Texarkana or the Dallas State Fair and Rodeo. We loaded and went to Nederland.

Monday, Pam and I rode to the fresh water canal about seven miles. We would lope about three or four hundred yards, then walk the horses about the same. We would ride them like this to keep them in shape. Tuesday, we loaded Gray Boy and Buck in the 14-foot stock trailer and took them to Uncle Jud's. Pam's mule, Star, was already there. We unloaded Buck and put him with the gray donkey, Pete, and two red donkeys. When Pete saw Buck he trotted up to see him. Pete now had a buddy. They all ran and played like kids. Pete and Buck acted like they hadn't seen each other in a long time. Tuesday evening Pam and I rode Star and Gray Boy to the sale barn in Kirbyville. We gave them a loose rein and they really covered some ground. Wednesday, we worked the sale and that evening, we rode back to Uncle Jud's. Thursday morning, Pam and I rode over to the Adam's land we had bought. T.J. was glad to see us. We visited and rode around the place to get a good look. Pam and I both decided we did not want to leave Star and Gray Boy at Uncle Jud's. Uncle Jud and Aunt Willie would be gone Wednesday and Thursday. They would be at the sale barn. Good, gaited saddle mules are hard to find and we liked having them in an eight-foot chain link fence at Nederland better. Friday evening, Harry and Arlene came out. Harry wanted to work on some two-wheel carts. They worked on two and added one foot to the front. I made wooden storage boxes, 12" x 12" x 36", and made lids for them. They stayed in their cabin that night and worked on them Saturday morning. Saturday evening, we all rode to the sale barn and back. Sunday morning we were sitting around talking when Clyde drove up and told us there is going to be a rodeo in De

Quincy. He is one of the pickup men and the rodeo contractor wanted him to find another. I told him about Harry, he was the pickup man at Jasper and his wife rode the donkey in the barrel racing. The contractor wanted him to find out if we all could be there. He paid each pickup man $50 a show for him and his horse. The rodeo was going to be a one-day show the next Saturday. It would start at 1 p.m. and go till it's over; we should get home by dark. Harry looked at me and I nodded my head, then Arlene and Pam nodded. So we all said we would go. Clyde said to tell Porter and anyone else we could think of. Clyde said he would meet us here about 9 a.m. next Saturday. We said we would be ready. Harry and Arlene went home after Clyde left.

Monday morning, Pam and I rode Sandy and Dusty to the sale barn in Beaumont and gave them a good workout. We saw Joe Johnson at the café and told him about the De Quincy rodeo. I asked him to call E.C. and tell him. He is a calf roper and just started dogging. Then Herb came in with his wife, Dot. We told them to sit with us and I introduced Pam to them. Herb and Dot said they would go to De Quincy. Herb is a saddle bronc rider and Dot is a barrel racer and trick rider. We decided we would all meet here at the sale barn next Saturday at 9 a.m. We told Herb and Dot to come see us. Pam and I rode Sandy and Dusty back home. Tuesday, Pam and I loaded Gray Boy and Star and drove to Uncle Jud's. Uncle Jud told us that Pete and Buck hadn't been 20 feet apart since Buck got here. Tuesday after dinner, we rode Star and Gray Boy to the sale barn. Porter came up right after we got there. He had Mike and Jeff with him. We walked over to where Dub was set up to shoe horses. I told both of them about the De Quincy Rodeo. They were glad to know about it. We worked the sale and after it was over, Pam and I rode back to Uncle Jud's. Thursday, we loaded Star and Grey boy and drove to Nederland. Friday morning, Pam and I rode Sandy and Dusty to the Beaumont sale barn. Just as we rode up and tied our horses Tom Smith hollered, telephone! It was Norm; he wanted to tell me about a rodeo at Waco. It was Thursday night, Friday night, and two shows on Saturday. Then they would go to Big Springs for the 4th of July rodeo. It was on Wednesday night, Thursday night, Friday night, and two shows on Saturday. Then we could come back to Jacksonville for the next Wednesday, Thursday, Friday and two shows on Saturday. Norm said they needed us to make the show. Most everyone else would be at Pecos for a bigger rodeo. I told Norm we would try to make it. Also, I would try to get some more cowboys to go also. Joe and Herb drove up about them and I told them about the rodeos. They seemed real glad and wanted to plan to go. I told them we could go to De Quincy this Saturday and come back home and leave next Monday and go to Waco. They said it was okay with them. We all decided to meet here at the sale barn about 9 a.m. so we could all drive together. Pam and I then rode back home. That evening Harry and Arlene came out. We loaded all our tack and checked out everything.

Saturday morning we loaded our horses and Pedro and drove to the sale barn in Beaumont. We got there right after 7:30 a.m. and ate breakfast, and soon everyone got there and we headed for De Quincy. We got to there about 11 a.m. There were not many cowboys there, so I entered the bareback, and saddle bronc, and steer dogging. I won first in bareback. I won second in saddle bronc. Herb was there and he won first in the saddle bronc. My steer dog fell (one foot under his body), so I didn't place in the dogging. Herb's wife, Dot, won the barrel racing. Pam won second (her horse was just three years old and was still learning). Arlene won 4th in barrel racing and the crowd all stood for her and Pedro. Harry and Clyde were the pickup men. We got home before dark. Monday, we all met at the sale barn in Beaumont about 8 a.m. We ate breakfast and soon everyone showed up. Herb and Dot were driving a Ford ranch wagon. They had a 5' x 12' horse trailer with a large tack and saddle compartment. Dot had her sixteen-year-old sister, named Cindy, with them, and she introduced her to us. She was out of school for the summer and wanted to go along. Herb and Dot were in the lead. Joe was second with his panel truck. Pam and I were third and Dub, the horse-shoer, was last. We got to Waco in the afternoon and picked a place so we could all camp together. Brownie Ford was there. He had his leopard appaloosa mule in his trailer. He unloaded his mule, which was about 50 inches tall, and then cleaned his trailer so he could sleep in it. Most everyone does this now. I locked two stalls so I would have a place for Sandy and Dusty. I entered the saddle bronc and the dogging. Pam entered the barrel racing and hazed in the dogging on Dusty. Pam made about three hundred in barrel racing and hazing.

CHAPTER 8

MONDAY MORNING, WE ALL LOADED UP and headed for Big Spring, Texas. Brownie joined in our group. When we got to Big Spring, it was late at night. We just parked and unloaded our horses, staked them out and went to bed. Next morning, we all parked in our group. Then Will and his wife Connie parked next to us; he still had the '46 Ford panel truck and the 4' x 10' trailer, and Socks the black dogging horse I had sold him. Will told me he had made more than he paid for Socks. Then Todd and his wife drove up. They still had the dogging team I sold them. Curtis drove up also, they were all traveling together. Will wanted to know what we were using for a hazing horse. I showed him Sandy and Dusty. I told him Dusty is a hazing horse and barrel horse. Pam barrel races on him. Will told me Connie had sold her barrel horse. Pam said Connie could use Dusty to barrel race, one could go first and the other could go last. Connie looked surprised. Will told Connie that is the kind of folks we were. I was the fellow that helped when Babe dropped dead. Then Pam told Connie she could haze for Will in the dogging. Again, Connie looked surprised. She turned to Will and asked where did you find these kinds of folks? Pam and Connie have been good friends ever since.

The next day, the fellow I saw in Jasper drove up. He parked way off by himself with another fellow. He was the one with the patch over one eye. Brownie Ford parked with us. He had his guitar and I had my Stella guitar. We would set around and pick and Brownie would sing. He taught me to pick along, and Pam and I would sing backup. I never knew a person who knew so many songs. We picked and sang songs every evening. Other cowboys would gather around and watch us. One evening, the rodeo producer heard us picking and came over. He asked

Brownie if he would sing before the rodeo and entertain the audience and asked what he would charge. Brownie said let's see how the audience likes us first. Well, the audience really liked us. Pam and I sang backup. Brownie told the rodeo producer we would perform before each show, twenty-five for himself and twenty-five for Pam and me. The contractor said that would be fine. (I would have done it for free.) Brownie told us to always try to get money when you perform. I entered the saddle bronc and dogging. I had Homer, Norm, and Joe using Sandy in the dogging and Pam hazed for us. Will had one fellow mounted on Socks and this fellow had a friend with a roping horse that he also hazed on. Everything went well; Sandy acted like a seasoned dogging horse for a three-year-old. Everyone that used him had placed on him. Saturday morning we were all setting around with Brownie and we were going over some songs to sing. Dot's sixteen-year-old sister, Cindy, was there also. Buck, the fellow with the patch over his eye, came riding by on his black dogging horse. When he saw Cindy he made a bad remark about her. Herb was there and told him he shouldn't talk that way to her, that she is just sixteen. Buck told him he would say anything he wanted to. Herb said, "No, you can't." Buck said, "Yes, I can and you can't stop me." Herb said, "Yes, I can." Buck said, "No, you can't." The argument grew all afternoon. Brownie told us to stay out of it, this wasn't good. All through the afternoon rodeo, things got worse. Buck was one of the judges. Herb had already ridden his bronc in the last show. Buck would have claimed he had missed his horse out of the chute. By now, Buck was carrying his pistol in his belt and he didn't care who saw it. When the bareback riding started, Buck still had his pistol in his belt. He had a denim jacket over it, but you could see he had it on him. Buck and Herb had been looking at each other all evening. Herb knew Tommy had a .38 in his car, so when the bareback riding started, Herb went and got the .38. When the last bareback bronc came out, Herb went into the rodeo arena with the .38 in his hand. Buck saw him walking towards him. Buck went for his gun. Herb fired the .38, but missed the first shot. But he hit Buck in the chest the next two shots and Buck fell to the ground. The first shot that Herb fired hit a fellow in the arena and he fell to the ground. Pam and I were setting on Sandy and Dusty at the far end of the arena. There were no bleachers and we were right up at the fence. I had been talking to a deputy sheriff who had been standing there.

When I saw Herb walking in the arena, I told the deputy to watch this. The deputy said, well, we've got an old west shoot out for entertainment. I said, no, this is the real thing. I gave Pam the reins to Sandy. The deputy and I climbed the fence and ran out to Buck. Soon the ambulance drove into the arena and picked up Buck and the other fellow and took them to the hospital. I think the crowd thought it was entertainment. I knew it was real. The rodeo went on as if it was an act. They took Herb to the police station. They took his statement and called a judge. The deputy and I made statements also. We didn't know what had happened to Herb till the next morning, Sunday. The deputy that I had been talking to came out to the rodeo arena and told us that Buck and the other fellow were both dead on arrival at the hospital. The judge ruled self-defense and the fellow's parents did not press charges. Herb said he was going home and try to put all this behind him. Pam and I and Joe Johnson told Herb and Dot to come see us, that it was you or him, and we held nothing against him. Pam and I were talking with Joe and Brownie and Dub. I noticed Will and the fellow that used his black horse, Socks, in the dogging were talking. In a little while, Will motioned for Pam and me to come over. Will and Connie walked towards us. Will said Don wanted to buy Socks and his trailer. I said, well, sell them to him. Will said what will I do for a dogging horse. I told him I would sell him Sandy and Dusty. Will asked what he should ask for Socks and the trailer. "Well," I said, "I sold him to you for $4000, and you have won that much already. You should ask $4500 for Socks and saddle, and you should ask $500 for the 4 x 10 trailer." Will went back over and told Don $5000 for Socks and the trailer. Don said, okay he'd take it. Don was going to El Paso, then to Scottsdale, then on to California, then on to Oregon. Then Will and Connie came back and asked my price for our complete rig. I priced them like this:

Sandy is just a three-year-old and is still learning	$4000
Dusty, same age, barrel and hazing horse	$3500
5' x 14' rodeo trailer	$1300
With bed and foot locker	$1400
'47 Ford Panel Truck – Deluxe towing package	$1600
This comes to:	$10,500
I will take the '46 Ford Panel Truck and allow trade of	- $800
Balance	$9700

Will agreed, he said he planned to go from here to El Paso to a rodeo, then to Scottsdale, Arizona, then to Albuquerque, New Mexico. They would not have time to make Texarkana, but they would see us at the Dallas State Fair and Rodeo. Will and Connie started loading their things in the truck and trailer. Tommy and Homer came up. Homer started telling me about the pickup horses Tommy had. They were wore out and needed to rest, and did I know of any good pickup horses. I told them I had a pair of sorrel horses about fifteen hands tall and asked how many they needed, and when they needed them. Tommy said they needed them for the Jacksonville rodeo, and asked how much they would cost? I told Tommy they were $600 each. I could go home and get the pair and have them at Jacksonville Tuesday. Also, I guaranteed the horses. He could try them out at Jacksonville and if he didn't want them, all he would be out was the feed. Tommy said, go get them.

When they left, Pam and I went to the pay phone. I called the Star Ranch. Matt answered the phone. I asked what he had that would make a dogging team. Matt said he had traded some mares for some good gray horses, and thought they had just what I wanted. I told Matt I would be there in about eight hours, I was in Big Spring. I would be driving a '46 panel truck. I had sold my complete rig. Matt said, come on, they would be looking for us. We told Joe and Dub, the horseshoer, we would see them at Jacksonville. We got in the truck, that I used to own and had taken in trade, and we drove hard. We each drove 2-3 hours, and then the other would drive. It took Pam and me over eight hours to the Star Ranch. Matt was looking for us. I told Matt, the first thing we need to do is take a shower. He laughed and pointed at one of the cabins. We each took a shower and lay down and rested about thirty minutes. Later, I told Matt I didn't have a trailer and asked if he could he deliver a load to Nederland. Matt said he and his dad could deliver the horses in the morning; they could leave out early and make it back in one day. He wanted to see my place. Matt said he hoped I could buy ten head. I said, let's go see the horses.

The first horse I picked was a gray horse; 55" tall, half-Welsh and half-Quarter horse and very fast. The second horse was a gray horse, 60" tall, half-Welsh and half-Quarter horse also very fast. This would make a good dogging team. Matt said this is the pair he told me about. The price on them is $300 each. I said that was ok. The next pair was two gray horses about 62 inches. Matt said the man they got this pair from said they were half-Welsh and Quarter horse type, with 1/8 Percheron. They could run, but not fast enough for dogging or calf roping. The next six horses were also gray, ¼ Quarter horse, ¼ Percheron, and half-Welsh. Two horses were over 56", two horses were 55", one horse was 54", and one horse was 53". The only one they didn't work was the first pair for $300 each. The 62" horses were $200 each. The last six were $150 each. Matt commented that we had picked the best of the horses. We added all the horses plus $75 delivery charge = $1975.00. I wrote a check on the Circle W account to the Star Ranch.

The next morning we all got up about four a.m. and loaded the horses. I told Matt I wanted to stop in Livingston and see if the saddle shop had any more saddles. We got to the saddle shop just as he was opening. He had two roping saddles that were used. He had one used, good, riding saddle. I bought all three and put them in the panel truck. We got to Nederland before 11 a.m. We unloaded the horses and we showed them around. Dad came out and I introduced him to Matt and his dad, Bill. Matt and Bill left soon and headed back home. I showed Dad the horses and he wanted to know what we were going to do with all those horses, and then laughed. Then he wanted to know where my truck and trailer and horses were. I told him I had sold them to Will and his wife and took my '46 Ford panel truck back in trade. Also, we had to leave in a little while and go to Newton – I had to deposit a check for the whole rig I sold Will. We had to leave in the morning and go to Jacksonville as I had sold the two sorrel horses to the Diamond S Rodeo Company for pickup horses. I needed to call Clyde and see if he could haul the sorrel horses, since I was hauling the gray horses. I called Clyde and asked him if he would use my '46 panel truck and my new 5' x 10' horse trailer to haul the sorrel horses. I would pay him $50, plus $25 traveling expenses. He could leave his truck here and bring my truck and trailer back here. Clyde said he wasn't doing anything and when did we want to leave. I told him we could leave about 9 a.m. in the morning, that it would take about 4-5 hours to drive it. He could sleep in the panel truck and drive back Wednesday. Clyde said ok, he would see us about 8 a.m. in the morning. I told my folks we would be back about 5-6 p.m. Dad wanted to know if we would eat supper with them. We both said, sure.

We got in the '46 truck and headed to Newton. We got the check deposited in the bank and didn't stop to visit anyone since we wanted to get back home. Mother had a big supper ready when we got home. I told them all that had happened at Big Spring, about selling the truck, trailer, and horses. The next morning, Clyde drove up about 8 a.m. He put his truck under the shed. We had the 5 x 10 trailer hooked to '46 panel truck. We had the 5 x 14 stock trailer hooked to the '47 pickup. We put the gray horses in the 5 x 10 trailer since they were the lightest in weight. We put the larger sorrel pickup horses in the 5 x 14 trailer. Both trailers had surge brakes on them. We got to Jacksonville about 4 p.m. Homer and Norm were glad to see us. Homer had four stalls reserved for the horses. The first thing I did was take all four horses over to Dub and let him trim their hoofs. When Dub got through, Homer and Norm saddled the sorrel horses and rode them around. Tommy came up – he liked the horses. I told Tommy I had a pair of gray horses also. They had a little more class than the sorrels. Tommy said he would keep it in mind.

The rodeo started Wednesday night at 8 p.m., then Thursday night, Friday at 1 p.m. and 8 p.m., Saturday 1 p.m. and 8 p.m. The gray horses did great. Everyone that used them made money on them. I named the gray 55" horse, Chunky. I named the gray 60" horse, Skip. After the rodeo, Tommy came by and wrote me a check for $1200 for both sorrel horses. He said he hoped we were going to Texarkana. I told him we were planning on it. Clyde had left Wednesday and went back home. Sunday morning we all loaded up and headed home. I told Dub to come by, I had some horses that needed hoofs trimmed. He said, how about Monday morning. I said that would be fine that I was going to Kirbyville Tuesday. Monday morning, Dub showed up. He started with the gray horses first. He trimmed hoofs till after dinner. Dub said he was going to Kirbyville also; he might get some hoof work there. Monday after dinner, I called Big "T" Trailers in Mesquite. I told Mr. T I had sold my 5' x 14' rodeo trailer and wanted to know if he had another. He said he had two ready with a primer coat, ready to paint any color, and they were 16 ft long. I told Mr. T I was going to a Ford dealer and see what color the 1949 models would have. I didn't want a '48 model, the '49 models would be out in about a month, I would wait on a '49. I would check on colors and get back with him. Mr. T said the 5' x 16' is like the one he sold me.

Tuesday morning, Pam and I went to Newton. I drove the '47 Ford pickup; it sure rode better than the '46 panel truck. The '46 was a custom; the '47 was a deluxe. I made a deposit in the Circle W account, then went to Uncle Jud's and visited with him. We didn't ride Grey boy and Star, since we had things to do. After dinner, we went to the Ford dealer in Kirbyville. I told Chuck, the dealer, I wanted a 1949 deluxe panel truck. Chuck told me the '49 would be out the last part of September. I told him, I would wait. I got this '47 deluxe and it rides better. I wanted a towing package, four-speed transmission, with a granny gear, two-bucket seats. Chuck told me he could get a long wheelbase, it has eight feet behind the seats. I said good, I want it. Chuck told me he could get chrome wheels and hubcaps, chrome grill guard, two-speed windshield wipers. I said, fine. Then, he told me he could get a bench seat that bolts down behind the front seats, and he can get two sliding windows on the passenger side and it had screen wire over it so bugs couldn't get in which was good. I told Chuck, I wanted everything on it. If they had anything else, tell them to put it on it. I asked about colors. He showed us a cream color. We both liked the cream color. Chuck said, he would call the factory and place the order and find out when they could ship it. In a few minutes, Chuck came back and said the truck should be here the middle of September. I told him, fine, we would be in Texarkana rodeo and to hold it till we got here. I asked the color number of cream so I could call and have our trailer painted the same color. Chuck told me the number and said I could call from here. I called Big "T" Trailers in Mesquite and told him the paint number, and to let me know when the trailer is ready. He said, okay.

We then went to the auction barn to work the sale. Porter was there and I told him about Big Spring and Jacksonville. Then Herb and Dot drove up. We waved them over. They got out and Porter asked Dot if she could work in the office – they needed some help. Then he asked Herb if he would help out with the pen work and they both said, yes. After the sale, Pam and I asked Herb and Dot if they would like to ride horses with us. Sometimes we ride to the Beaumont sale on Fridays, eat dinner at the café, and ride back when the sale starts. We have plenty of horses, no need to bring any. They both said, maybe, it would sure be something to do. I told them about the ten gray horses we had bought. They both looked surprised. They said they would like to see them. We told them to come out Thursday evening after dinner, we would be there. Herb said, okay. Thursday, they came out and we showed them all the horses. When they saw the sorrel horse, Snip, Herb said, he looks like the horse I sold to Will and Connie. I told them he came from the same ranch, that Dusty and Skip had the same sire. Pam had started training Snip on barrels, and I believe he just as fast. Herb said they would like to ride to the Beaumont sale with us. We both said, great. We would leave about 9 a.m. It is about a two-hour ride. We could eat dinner, visit around, and ride back.

Then Pam asked Dot if she would like to run the barrels on Snip. The barrels are all set up. Dot said, yes. I went and got my stopwatch while they saddled Snip. He ran real well. Pam told Dot she could ride Snip to the sale tomorrow. Dot smiled and said, okay. We visited a while and they said they would see us in the morning. The next morning, they got here about 8:30 a.m. Pam let Dot ride Snip. The rest of us rode gray horses. We let the dogging team rest. I asked as we rode along if they would like to go to the Alexandria rodeo the middle of August. Herb said they were planning to go and asked if we were going. I said, yes, it starts on the 15th of August, Thursday, and ends on Saturday, the 17th. We could all meets here or the Beaumont sale barn. We can do like when we went to Waco and all travel together. I think Joe is going. Dot smiled, Cindy would like that, also E.C., Dub, Porter and family. We will probably leave on Wednesday morning and Porter would drive up Thursday morning. We rode back after dinner, and Herb and Dot both said they enjoyed the ride and visit.

Tuesday morning, the Big "T" Trailer Company called and said the rodeo trailer was ready. I told them we would come to pick it up since he wasn't bringing any trailers this way. We would be there Thursday a.m. Tuesday evening about 4 p.m., Mr. T. called. He said he had sold two more trailers and he could have my trailer at the Kirbyville sale barn Thursday a.m. about 6 or 7 a.m. I told him, fine, and to tell me how much to make the check for and I would give the driver the check. Mr. T. said material had gone up and cost of living also, so $1300 for a new horse trailers. I said, ok, I would give the driver a check. Tuesday p.m. after Mr. T. called Pam and I drove up to Newton and visited with Uncle Jud and Aunt Willie. After dinner, we drove to the sale barn. Uncle Jud said he would be there later, that Aunt Willie was not going. We got to the sale and Dub was there. We were talking with him and Porter drove up. We told Porter Willie was not going to be here, she wasn't feeling well. Then Herb and Dot drove up. Porter asked Dot if she would help in the office, and would Herb help in the back. They both said, okay. I told everyone about the trailer we had bought and it would be here Thursday a.m. We worked the sale, but nothing came through I wanted. Porter bought a couple of young steers that might make dogging steers. Thursday morning, we woke up about daylight, went to the café and ate breakfast. When we came back, the man with the trailer was driving up. We unhooked our trailer and looked it over. Our trailer had windows in it that could be open in the summer and closed in the winter. I gave the driver the envelope with the check inside. The driver then left to deliver the other trailers. We hooked our new trailer to the '47 pickup and drove to Nederland.

We went back to the furniture store and bought a new folding bed for the horse trailer. Then went to the carpet store and bought some carpet and went back home and fitted it in the trailer. Pam and I were talking and I said maybe we should let Chunky and Skip stay here, and maybe take a pair of gray horses to Alexandria. Let's go out and take a better look at the six gray horses we just bought. For now, we hadn't named the six horses, so I called them, G-53, G-54, G-55, and G-56 (G for Gray). G-54 looked like he might be fast than Matt thought. Then Pam said G-56 might be faster also. Friday morning, we rode all six gray horses. Pam and I would saddle two gray horses, G-54 and G-56. We rode in the training arena, backed the pair in as if we were going to do some steer dogging. We hollered and they busted out of the chute like they had done this before. Pam said we just might have a pair of dogging horses here. Then we tried another pair, until we had ridden all the horses. The only one that didn't try very hard was G-53, but that was okay, he'd make a good carthorse. Pam and I both agreed to take G-56 and G-55 to Alexandria and save Chunky and Skip for Texarkana. We worked on that pair that evening.

About 6 that evening, Norm and Tom Smith drove up. Tom wanted to know about my dogging arena. He had fourteen young steers that he had at the sale barn, and he said that the Diamond S Rodeo needed some dogging steers for the Texarkana rodeo. They need to be run through a chute and run in an arena so they would know what to do. He wanted to know what I would charge to train the young steers. I told him after all he had done and helped me, I would not think of charging anything. Besides, I got some young horses that needed some training. Then I asked Tom if he needed any more steers. Porter has some and Joe may have some in his pasture. Norm said that they would need at least thirty steers; Tommy had some but not enough. I asked Tom when he wanted to train the steers. Tom asked, how about tomorrow, Saturday. He said why didn't I call Porter and Joe to bring what steers they had and be here about 9 a.m. in the morning. I told Tom, ok, wait here and I'll call right now. I called Joe and Porter. They both said they would be here. Then I called Herb and Dot. They said, that would be good and they would bring Cindy. Tom and Norm left; said they would see us in the morning. That evening, Harry and Arlene came out. I told them all about tomorrow. Harry said, that should be fun, he could haze on Bill. I said sure, we would need lots of help to run 25 to 30 steers. Harry and Arlene spent the night.

The next morning, we started getting ready. By nine o'clock we had thirty-two steers in the pens. Tom had 14, Porter had 6, and Joe brought 10 head, but he didn't bring Jet, he didn't have room. I told him I thought I had plenty of horses Pam asked Dot if she wanted to ride Snip. Dot smiled and said, sure, put Porter on Cody. Porter didn't bring his horses since I told him I had plenty. The first run, we just ran the steers (we didn't get down on them). We all had a good time. Tom Smith bought all the steers. He paid the pound price and took them back to the sale barn pens. Nothing much went on till it was time to go to Alexandria. Tuesday, before the Alexandria rodeo, we all met at the Kirbyville sale barn. After the sale Wednesday, we left for Alexandria. Porter and his family stayed, they would leave Thursday a.m. Herb and Dot parked with Pam and me. Dub and Joe also parked close by. We roped off a place for Porter and family. Two fellows parked next to Joe on the other side. They were from south Louisiana. They rode bulls and dogged steers. They asked Joe if he knew of a dogging team they could get mounted on. Joe told them about our team and brought them over. I told them my team was young, they were just three-year-olds.

I would mount them if they wanted. I had three beside myself. They both said ok. Although we had never met, we knew some of the same people. Everyone that used the pair of grays made money. After the one p.m. show, the LeBlanc brothers (Jody and Toby) were talking with us. They wanted to know if I would sell the gray pair of dogging horses. I asked if they wanted the saddles also. They said, yes. They had a new 12 foot stock trailer and needed the horses and saddles. I told them the pair was still young, but were learning fast. I would sell the horses and two saddles and tack for $3000 for all. If they were seasoned and well trained I would ask more; also, I had another pair at home. They said they could buy them tonight after the show. I told them I would not charge them a mounted fee. They should make that much on the pair the next two or three months. They said they would take them. We had become good friends and knew more about each other. I asked what they did for a living and they said they were rice farmers. They had a good season and would not start up again till March. I asked if they were going to Texarkana, where we were going. Jody asked when it was. I told them it starts on Wednesday, September 1, and we would leave on Sunday, the 8th. We were all going to meet at the Kirbyville sale barn on Saturday, the day before. They were welcome if they wanted to travel with us. They looked kind of puzzled, and then said they would try to be there.

Friday, September 7th, Tom Smith called. He said Tommy had called, and wanted the steers, but he wanted to see the steers run. Tommy and Norm and Homer were all in town and would leave here and take the steers straight to Texarkana. I told Tom to bring the steers Saturday morning. The next morning Harry and Arlene came out early. We started saddling horses. In a little while, two long trailers drove up. I had the double gates open. When Homer saw the pair of gray horses, he asked about them. I told him that was the pair I had told him about, and offered for him to ride them and see how they handle. Tommy didn't say anything. He just looked them over real good. We ran all the steers, and when it was over, Tommy asked how much for the gray horses, and how much for using the pens. I told him the gray horses were $750 each and I would not charge anything for running the steers if he bought the grays or not. Tommy thanked me and Tom Smith thanked me. Then Tommy wrote me a check for the horses. They put the grays up front in one of the trailers and put the steers in both of the trailers to balance the loads. Homer asked if we were going to Texarkana. I told him we are going to Kirbyville this evening and would leave Sunday morning. Homer said he and Norm would leave from Beaumont early in the morning. He said Tommy was going back to Austin and get the rodeo stock going from there. That evening Pam and I drove to Kirbyville. We put Chunky and Skip in pens. Then Joe drove up with Jet and put him in a pen. Dub was right behind him. Then Herb and Dot drove up, too. Dot had her older barrel horse with them, and put him in a pen. We all went to the café and ate supper. Porter wasn't going since he had to stay and operate the sale barn. The next morning, Pam and I led the way. About six hours later, we got to Texarkana. Homer and Norm were already there. They had left Beaumont at 3 a.m. It was cooler that time of the morning.

CHAPTER 9
Texarkana Rodeo

MONDAY AFTERNOON, JODY AND TOBY LEBLANC drove up. They entered the bull riding and the dogging. I entered the saddle bronc and dogging, and Pam entered the barrel racing. We were there till September the 22nd, on Sunday, 12 days, two shows a day. Altogether, Pam and I made a little over $1200. Monday morning, we all left for home. I told everyone we would turn at Jasper and go to Newton. Uncle Jud and Aunt Willie were looking for us. We spent the night with them. Next morning we were sitting on the front porch when T.J. Adams and his wife drove up. T.J. wanted to know if I was still interested in buying the rest of his land. I told T.J. that I wanted the place and they could live on it as long as they wanted and asked how much they wanted. T.J. said there were 150 acres and the house and he wanted $12,000 for it. I asked if all the minerals and timber went with it and he said yes. So I said let's go to the courthouse and have the paperwork done and have it put in the deal that they can live on it as long as they want. We went to the courthouse and then to the bank and I wrote a check on the Circle W Enterprise account. I thanked T.J. for letting me buy the place and Pam and I went back to Uncle Jud's. While we were at the bank, I deposited the check that Tommy paid me for the pair of gray horses. He used the grays for carrying the Texas and U.S. flags. Also, they were used some for pickup horses.

Tuesday evening, we went to the sale barn. I told Porter all about the trip. Porter told me that Chuck called and said the '49 Ford deluxe panel truck was in. Pam and I walked over to the dealership. The truck was setting on the show room floor. The Truck had everything on it you could think of. I asked Chuck how much and he said $2495. I wrote him a check and we drove it back to the barn. I hooked the horse trailer to the new truck and pulled the new trailer with the dogging team. Pam drove the '47 pickup to Nederland after the sale. We got home and brought my folks up to date and showed them the new truck. They were glad we had bought the rest of the Adam's place. Thursday, after dinner, Herb called. He wanted to know if Snip was for sale and asked how much. I told him I would sell him to them for $2000. Herb said they would be right out if that was okay. I told him, sure, come on out. Herb said they didn't have to ride him, they knew all about him. They had Dot's younger sister, Cindy, with them. Dot said Cindy has all her grades up and will graduate next spring. They have talked to the teacher and the principal and got an okay to take off from school and go to the Dallas Rodeo. Dot and Cindy will both enter the barrel racing and they need another barrel horse. Herb wanted to know when we all would be leaving. I told them I thought we should leave early Saturday morning. We all could meet here Friday evening. Joe and Dub said they would be here. Herb said they would be here also and we could all leave from here. They would just leave Snip here and go ahead and give me a check for him. I said, ok, and I put Herb's check for Snip in a metal box. Friday evening, everybody drove up, and we set up for the night. I told my folks the rodeo ends on Thursday, the 31st. We would all leave Friday morning early and head for home. Saturday morning we all got ready and headed for Dallas State Fair and Rodeo. We got to the fairgrounds that afternoon, and picked a good place to set up camp for all of October.

Sunday, Will and Connie drove up. I waved them over and they parked next to us. I told Will he had better go lock a couple of stalls for Sandy and Dusty. Will looked at me and said, "I don't have them anymore; I mounted a fellow at Cheyenne and at the end of the show he wanted to buy them. I really didn't want to sell them so I priced them at $5000, thinking he wouldn't buy them, but he said okay and wrote me a check. I kept my saddle, truck and trailer." Then Will asked if I was booked up on this dogging team. I told him I would make room for him. Then Pam asked Connie if she needed to use Skip, the gray horse, in the barrel racing. Connie said she sure did, we can check with the bookkeeper and try to not have us both riding in the same show. At the end of the show, everyone that used Chunky made money. Pam and I, altogether, made a little over $4000. Then Will and Connie wanted to buy Chunky and Skip, the pair of grays. I told Will I would sell them to him for $8000 for the pair and not charge him a mounting fee. Will said that was about what he was thinking and wrote me a check. I told him to make the check to Circle W Enterprise.

Friday morning, November 1st, we all left for home and got in just before dark. Saturday, we took it easy and rested. Harry and Arlene came out. I brought them up to date on what all had happened. We all walked over to where the gray horses were. We still had four of the six that I bought at the Starr ranch. One horse was 57" high and one horse was 54" high. I told Pam they might make a dogging team. She said it would be worth a try. We named them Salty and Steeler. Harry and Arlene asked about going to Uncle Jud's and ride in the woods. I told them I would see Uncle Jud Wednesday, he works at the sale barn for Porter on Wednesday. He has a contract to clean the pens on Thursday and Friday. I told them we have four big donkeys now to farm with and they all work or ride. We have a pair of red donkeys, one gray donkey, and one buckskin donkey. We don't have to haul anything to ride on. Y'all can come out Friday evening, and we can leave early Saturday morning, and come back Saturday evening. I will talk to Uncle Jud Wednesday. I will call you Thursday night to let you know. Tuesday morning, Pam and I drove the '47 pickup to Kirbyville. I talked to Uncle Jud about going riding next Saturday. He said, sure, he would barbecue some beef. Tuesday evening we drove back to the sale barn, and saw that a few cows were brought in.

We worked the sale Wednesday and went home Wednesday evening. I called Harry and told him that Uncle Jud said to come on up. Harry said they would come out Friday evening and spend the night and we could leave early Saturday. We did leave out early Saturday, and stopped and ate breakfast at the café. We got there about 9 a.m. and rode till about 11 a.m. We went in the '49 panel truck; it has a bench seat behind the front seats. We told them about buying the rest of the Adams place. After dinner we rode all over the Adam's place. They really liked it and were glad we had bought the place. Saturday evening we drove back to Nederland. Sunday morning we looked at the last four gray horses. We had one steel gray horse 57" high, one steel gray 54" high, one light dapple gray 55" high, and one light dapple gray 53" high. The 57" steel gray was named "Steeler." The 54" steel gray we named Salty." We looked Salty and Steeler over and it looked like they could make a dogging team.

After dinner, Pam and I saddled Salty and Steeler. We backed them in the dogging box and broke them out. The first time, they didn't know what was going on. The next time we jumped them out they did a lot better. Pam would hold Steeler back so that Salty was always about two feet ahead. Then Pam rode Steeler in a trot on the barrels a couple of times. Then we stopped for the day. Monday morning we saddled Salty and Steeler and rode to the Beaumont sale barn. We would lope them three or four hundred yards and then walk them a ways. We needed to get them in shape for rodeoing. Tuesday morning, we left early and drove the '47 pickup to Newton. We wanted to visit with Uncle Jud and Aunt Willie. When we got to Bleakwood, no one was out, so we drove on. We got about three miles from Bleakwood when Pam saw a man putting up a "For Sale" sign. We stopped and asked him about the land. He said it was 50 acres in a rectangle shape. It is 5 acres wide on the highway and 10 acres deep, and then there is a 3 acre tract joining on the North, one acre on the highway and 3 acres deep (the old way for an acre is 210 feet x 210 feet). He said about 20 acres in the back has a small creek and woods. About 30 acres in front is all gravel. I asked if all the mineral rights go with it and the timber. He said, yes, and I asked how much for the 53 acres. He said since it is mostly gravel and will hardly grow weeds, he wants $3250 for it. Then I asked if he had the deed to the land with him. He said yes, the deed is in the car, and asked if I had the money to buy it. I said yes, and let's go to the courthouse and transfer the title. We got to the courthouse and they had the paperwork ready in about thirty minutes. I wrote him a check for the land on the Circle W account. He looked at the check, and asked who Circle W Enterprise is and who owns it. I told him he was looking at the President and Vice-President. He looked kind of startled, and then said ok. He went his way and we drove on the Uncle Jud's.

Uncle Jud asked where we had been, that he was looking for us sooner. I told him about buying the land. He said he knew the place, it is all gravel and it won't even grow weeds. I hope you didn't throw your money away. I told him I hoped I didn't throw my money away, too. We visited a while and after dinner Pam and I left for the sale barn, and on the way we stopped at the tract of land. It had a six-inch steel pipe on each corner, filled with concrete. Pam had not said anything about the land. She said, "I know you've got an idea about the land, so you might as well tell me." I smiled and said I think we can sell the gravel on it and make more than we paid. Then she smiled and said, "I thought you had something in mind when we bought it." I said, "We probably won't do anything with it till next year but I do want to ride over it and take a good look at it as soon as we can." Pam said that would be good.

As we drove by Ed Brown's office, he had an orange flag out in front. That is a signal that he wants us to stop – this is something we worked out. We parked the pickup and went in. He was glad we saw the flag signal. He and Mrs. Brown wanted to ride over the 1500 acres back of Uncle Jud's and wanted us to go along and show him and Mrs. Brown the land next Saturday. I told him we could saddle up and ride Saturday morning, come back to Uncle Jud's, eat dinner and ride Saturday evening. Harry and Arlene like to ride and I asked if it was okay for them to ride, too. They are the couple that rode on the cattle drive. He rode the buckskin horse and she rode Pedro, the gray donkey. Ed said sure, that would be good. He remembered them. We left Ed's office and said we would see them Saturday morning. Ed said he would give Uncle Jud some money to buy bar-b-que meat with. We worked the sale at Kirbyville and drove home Wednesday. I called Harry to ask if they wanted to go ride again. Brown said to come up. We would make a ride Saturday morning and Saturday evening. We would ride up on Friday evening. They said okay and Friday evening they drove up. We went in the '49 panel truck. It had a bench seat in it and four could ride in it good.

We got up early Saturday and fed all the stock. Ed and his wife drove up a little before 8am. They were ready to start riding. We started riding to the west. We came up on a six-inch pipe corner post. I told Ed this was a southwest corner post. Then we crossed the creek, it was a little over two-foot deep. Harry was riding Buck and I don't think he knew about creeks. He didn't want to cross. Arlene was riding Pete and he knew all about creeks. When we all started across the creek and Buck saw Pete cross the creek, Buck went in, too. We rode on north and I noticed Ed was looking at the timber. In a while, we came upon anther pipe. It was painted orange like the other one. We rode back and forth and we covered about half by 11am. We headed back to Uncle Jud's. He had bar-b-que ready. We unsaddled the donkeys and the mules and put out some fed. After dinner, we saddled up again and started where we stopped for dinner. We rode north till we came to the property line. Then we turned and east three or four hundred yards, and rode south and Ed was looking at the timber real close. I asked him if he was planning on cutting the timber soon. He said, yes, but it will probably be a year more till the cutters can get to it. We rode back to Uncle Jud's fence, turned east and were riding along the fence when we came to another six-inch pipe. Ed said this must be a corner post between your Uncle Jud's and the Adam's place. I said yes (I had not told him I had bought the Adam's place).

Ed looked across the fence and there were a lot of pine trees, 20-25 inches and real tall like the trees on the 1500 acres we were riding. He was very interested in the big trees. I told Ed that the Adam's place has been sold and asked if he knew about it? He said no, he did not know it. Harry and Arlene didn't say anything. We had all stopped and Ed was looking at the timber. Ed asked if we knew who had bought the place. Pam spoke up and said, yes, we knew who bought it. Ed asked could she find out if they would sell the timber. Pam asked Ed how soon he wanted to know. Ed said the sooner the better. Pam looked at me and asked if the Circle W would sell the timber. I said, well, the Circle W is real close with the Sabine River Timber Company and I am sure the Circle W Enterprise would not let anyone but the Sabine River Timber Company cut the timber. (Ed's wife knew that Ed had helped me form the Circle W Enterprise.) I looked at Ed's wife and she was grinning with a big smile. Harry and Arlene also were smiling. Ed looked at all of us, and he started smiling. Then he said, well, I don't get done very often, but I sure did this time. I told him Pam and I hoped we could do it this way. Then I told Ed that he could count on cutting the timber when he cut the other timber. We rode on and looked at more timber. Every time I would look at Ed, he was smiling.

We rode on back to Uncle Jud's. At supper, Ed told Uncle Jud how we did him on the timber. Then I told Ed about the 53 acres we had bought on Hwy. 87, and about it being all gravel. Ed said he was pretty sure we could sell gravel off of it. If he heard of anyone wanting gravel, he would tell him. After supper, Ed thanked us for showing them the timber, and he liked the way we did him on the Adams place. Of course, we all laughed. We left and got home about dark. Harry and Arlene stayed in their room that night. The next day, we rode and trained horses on the barrels. We decided we would go riding next Saturday. Harry and Arlene said, okay. Monday, Pam and I worked with Salty and Steeler, they were doing real good. Next Saturday, Harry and Arlene came out. We were getting ready to ride to the sale barn and back when it started raining. About noon the rain stopped and the sun came out. The weather was supposed to be good with a norther due in Sunday. We decided to go ahead and ride toward the sale barn.

Pam wanted to drive one of the two-wheel carts. I said, okay, I would drive the other. Pam said she would drive the small gray and I could drive the 55" gray. We harnessed the grays and Harry saddled Bill and Arlene saddled Pedro, the donkey. We headed to the sale barn. When we got to the fresh water canal about two miles from the sale barn, I looked to the north and saw there was a dark cloud and it was moving this way. I told Harry we had better turn around and head back. We had gone by a double gate and I noticed it was locked when we went by. Now it was shut, but was not locked. I asked Harry to look down the road and he said there were a couple of fellows walking this way and it looks like their truck had slid off the road. I got out and looked and said let's go see if they are all right. I opened the gate and we all went inside. Harry led my horse and cart and I shut the two gates. The two fellows were waving for us to go to them.

By now the norther was coming in and it was getting colder so we all put our jackets on. We rode to the fellows walking, but when we got to them we saw that it was not two fellows, it was E.C. and his wife. He had used my dogging horse at the De Quincy rodeo. They were sure glad to see us. E.C. remembered Harry and Arlene (she rode the donkey in the barrel racing). I told E.C. and his wife to take my cart and I would ride with Pam. They had not brought their coats and were both cold. I keep a pair of old jeans and extra coats in the storage boxes in the carts so I took the coats in Pam's cart and told them to put them on. E.C. wanted to know where we were going. I told him we were going to our place; it is about an hour or so ride. E.C. asked about getting his truck out to the road. I told him we could use horses to pull the truck out tomorrow, a wrecker would cost too much and I think it is not stuck too badly. When we got to our place, the women went inside and Pam lit the heater while we fellows unsaddled the horses. When we went inside, I told E.C. to call home and tell their kids they would be home soon and they would be driving a maroon pickup. E.C. wanted to know what plans I had to get the truck out. I told him I thought four horses could pull his truck on to the dirt road with saddles. I asked if his kids might want to come back and asked how old they were. E.C. said they would want to come back with them and he said his son is sixteen and his daughter is fourteen and both of them ride. I told him I had seven head of horses and mules and all of them will pull with saddle horn, but I think four head will pull the truck onto the road. We had eight people to ride, but only seven horses and mules. E.C. said he could bring his roping horse if it was all right to use my truck. I told him, sure, it has a four-speed transmission and it will pull it fine. (I did not use Salty and Steeler.)

Then E.C. asked how much this is all going to cost him. I told him nothing. He was in a bind and we were glad to help him out. I knew he had a much of cows, I just didn't know where. I showed him how to operate the heater in the truck, and asked him what time they would get here in the morning. E.C. said by the time they all got ready it would probably be about 9 a.m. I told him that would be fine, I had plenty of saddles, just bring one for his roping horse and to bring some strong rope if he had some. They got in the truck and left. The next morning we all got up and had the horses and mules ready. Harry rode Bill, Arlene rode Pedro, and Pam rode her saddle mule, Star. I put E.C.'s wife on Gray Boy, my saddle mule. I rode Cody, and I put Billy, E.C.'s son, on the 55" gray horse. I put the daughter on the 53" horse and E.C. rode his roping horse. We got to E.C.'s truck about 10:30 a.m. E.C.'s wife got in the truck. We fellows put our ropes on the stuck pickup. Pam was holding Grey boy. His wife started the truck and put it in first gear. All four horses worked real good and pulled the truck out and up on the dirt road and we all headed for the gate. We rode along and E.C.'s wife drove slowly along with us. When we were nearly home, E.C. saw the bar-b-que house and asked if we would all eat bar-b-que that he was buying. I told him he didn't have to do that, we didn't mind helping him. E.C. said he appreciated all the help and he would like to do this. I suggested he buy bar-b-que by the pound and buns, and take it to our place and w could make our own sandwiches. E.C. liked that idea and asked his wife if she would stop at the bar-b-que house and buy some for all of us. She thought that was a good idea. We rode on to the cabin. She bought the bar-b-que and buns and was right behind us when we got home.

When we got through eating, E.C. thanked all of us for helping again. I noticed E.C. and his family talking. In a moment, E.C. asked if I would sell the two horses his son and daughter had rode, and how much. I told him I would sell them and asked if he needed saddles and tack. He said, yes he needed all of it. I told him the 53" horse + tack … $350. The 55" horse is a good all around horse and the saddle is a roping saddle … total $550. Total for all was $900. E.C. said his son has been looking for a good horse and he would take both horses. I told him I guaranteed both horses and if he ever wanted a bigger horse than the 53" horse, I would take the horse in trade. E.C. loaded the horses, thanked us all again and left. Pam asked, "Well, what are we going to use for rodeo horses now?" "We can use Salty and Steeler," I said. "If we have to, we can use Salty to dog on and Steeler to haze and run barrels." Harry said they were both good horses and bet they could do the job. Harry and Arlene went home that evening.

Later that day, Pam asked why don't we call the Starr ranch and see if they have any good horses. I called and Bill answered the phone. I told him who I was and what I was looking for. Bill said he had just traded some mares for some geldings with his neighbor. They were the same bloodline that I had gotten before. They range in size from 53" to 60" or more and asked how many did I need? I told him eight to ten head. I did not have anything to pull a two-wheel cart and I need to train a dogging team and barrel horses. Bill said he was sure they had what I needed. I told him we could leave in the morning (Monday), and Bill said to load up and come on. I told him Pam and I would be there Monday after dinner. We would be driving a '49 Ford, cream color, and panel truck. Pam and I got ready so we could leave Monday morning. I told my folks we were going after a load of horses. We left out Monday morning, went to the bank there in Nederland and deposited E.C.'s check. I let Pam drive to Woodville and on to Livingston. We stopped at the saddle shop to see if he had any used saddles. He was glad to see us, and he had some saddles I liked. I bought five saddles, $50 - $75 – also bridles with hackamore bits. I like hackamore bits, horses don't seem to fight that kind of bit. He said he could have two more saddles ready tomorrow if I needed them. He showed me two roping saddles. I told him I would stop by about 9:30 a.m. in the morning. I paid him for the five saddles and put them in the panel truck. I did not bring a trailer.

We got to the ranch about 4 p.m. Matt was there and started showing us horses. He showed us two sorrel horses, half-Belgian and half-Welsh, kid gentle about 56" high. I told him I would take them. Then he took us to a big pen. There must have been 14-15 head in it, all gray and half Quarter horse. I picked three head, 54" to 56" high, then Pam and I picked three head, 58" to 61" high. These taller horses we would train for barrel racing and hazing in the dogging. We picked two more gray horses, 53" high that would work or ride. These two 53" horses we could use to pull a wagon or a two-wheel cart. Matt said the two 53" horses were kid gentle. The other six were gentle, but not kid gentle. Then we all went and ate supper. That night Bill has us stay in one of the guest cabins. We all got up about 4 a.m., ate breakfast and loaded the horses. We left about 5 a.m. and when we got to Livingston, we stopped at the saddle show. He had the other two saddles ready, so I paid him and we headed for Nederland. We got to Nederland about 11 a.m., unloaded the horses and Matt and Bill headed for home. We put the two sorrel horses in a pen together. The rest we put in the big pen behind our cabin. I called Porter and told him we could not get there today, we were too tired. We would see him Wednesday at the sale barn and bring him up to date. Porter said, okay and, he would see us tomorrow. Wednesday morning we drove the '47 Ford pickup to Kirbyville and told Porter about the horses. Dub was there and I also told him about the horses, and asked when he could come trim all their hoofs. Dub said he would be at our place in the morning. I said that would be okay and would see him then. After the sale, we drove back to Nederland. Thursday morning, Dub showed up about 8 a.m. He trimmed the two sorrel horses first, and then started on the gray horses. We would catch and halter the horses and have them ready to work on. Dub got through that evening. I paid him and asked if he was going to Beaumont tomorrow. Dub said, maybe – he was pretty tired.

Friday morning, Pam and I picked two of the gray horses and rode them to the Beaumont sale. E.C. and his wife were there. They came over to us and I showed him the gray horses and told him about the rest at home. Then Tom Smith walked up. He wanted to show us some young, dogging steers he had bought. He had ten head. When dogging type steers go through the sale, he buys them. Tom said he needed to run them through the dogging practice, like we had done before. I said good, I have some new horses and I need to try them out also, and when did he want to try them. Tom said, how about tomorrow? I said, that would be good, bring them about 8 or 9 a.m. We can run the steers, then run the barrels, and then run the steers again. Then I asked E.C. if he would like to bring his family and try the two horses he had got from me. E.C. and his wife said, well. They knew their son and daughter would like that.

Then Herb and Dot walked up and I asked them to come to our place in the morning, also. Dot said she could train Snip some, also. Dot said she had sold her trick riding horse, she didn't use him much. Then Joe Johnson came up and I invited him, also. He didn't have to bring his horse. We didn't have any calves, just some young steers. Joe said good, he would be there. Dot said they would bring Cindy, her younger sister. Saturday Harry and Arlene came out. We showed them the new horses and told them we were going to run some young steers and see how the horses would do. We started saddling horses. Soon, Tom showed up with the steers. We unloaded the steers and put them in the dogging chute. We would run the steers, get down on them and pull them to a stop. We did not throw them down, they were too young. Then we set up the barrels and tried the horses on the barrels. All the gray horses did well. Then we ran the steers again. This time the horses did better. Afterwards, Tom loaded his steers and took them back to the sale barn. Everybody had left but E.C. and his family, and Harry and Arlene. E.C. said he was going to do something he doesn't do very often. He had wanted to do something for helping when his truck was stuck. He handed Harry and I a piece of paper. We both looked at the note. It was permission for us to hunt and fish on his place. He told us there is about a three-acre lake close to where the truck was stuck, it has catfish and bream in it. If we hunt, to use only shotguns, and not to leave the shotgun shells on the ground, that cows will eat them, thinking they are range cubes. If we see any shells lying around, would we pick them up? Then he gave me a key to the gate and said when we go in to lock the gate behind us. We both thanked him and said we would take good care of his place. I told him I would get us each a key made, and get his key back to him. Then E.C. and his family left. They all thanked us for asking them to join in. We all thanked each other again. That evening we worked on the ten-foot, rubber-tired wagon. We got it all finished and ready. Sunday, Harry and Arlene went home.

Monday, Pam and I saddled the two sorrel horses and rode toward the sale barn. They rode good and traffic on the highway didn't bother them at all. We rode about halfway and turned around and headed back. I noticed a pickup was following us, staying way back. When we turned in at our gate, the pickup came on up and a man got out. He said he was looking for a couple of horses that were real gentle. He said that his two grandsons wanted to ride on the salt grass trail ride to Houston. Some of their friends are going. He wants two nice-looking horses that his boys would be proud of. I told him these two horses would be good horses for that and they were gentle for anyone. He asked what bloodline were these and how much. I said they were half-Welsh and half-Belgian, and they came off a ranch and would work or ride. The price is $400 each. He said he needed saddles and all. I told him I had saddles starting at $60 and up. He said he would go get his grandsons, and be back later. He got in his truck and thanked us and said he would see us later. I told Pam I didn't think he wouldn't be back. Pam said, well, I think he will be back and let his grandsons pick out their saddles. In about an hour and a half, Pam looked up the road and started grinning. I asked, well, what are you grinning about? She said there comes Grandpa with his grandsons. They got out and he introduced his grandsons, Willy and Billy Brady. They were nice-looking (they were twins). He said they were eighteen years old and had never ridden much. They want to ride with some friends on the salt grass trail ride to Houston. They needed some riding lessons, would I teach them and how much. Well, I said, I would try, but let's wait and see about how much. He wanted to know if we had any suggestions. He didn't want his grandsons to look like a couple of greenhorns, so his friends would not pick at them. First, I said, let's pick out the saddles. That would be a dead giveaway.

We went to the tack room. I picked out two roping saddles with rough out leather. I picked two hackamore bridles. I let the boys do the saddling. Then I showed them how to mount. I told them to ride a little. I could tell they hadn't ridden much, if any. Mr. Brady asked if we would help pick out clothes for them. I looked at Pam and she nodded her head. I said, okay, it is too late to go this evening. Tomorrow is Tuesday, could they go tomorrow? Mr. Brady asked his grandsons if they could go tomorrow. They said, yes. I told Mr. Brady the brand of clothes made a lot of difference. He agreed and said he knew I would know about that. I went to my rodeo trailer and got my chaps and showed them to Billy and Willy. I let them put them on and walk around. They had on an off-brand of blue jeans. I told Mr. Brady that the jeans were the wrong brand. He said he wanted us to pick their clothes. I told him to bring his checkbook tomorrow. He laughed and said, okay, and then he asked if he could leave the horses there tonight. I said, sure. Then he wanted to look at our 14-foot stock trailer; they would need a good trailer. I told him we slept in trailers all the time and so did a lot of other cowboys. Mr. Brady said he had a slide in camper for his ¾ ton truck and he would sleep in the truck and the boys could sleep in the trailer. Then he asked if I would sell this 14-foot trailer. I said, I guess so, but let me think about it. Then Billy and Willy walked up and handed me the chaps. I asked if they would like a pair of chaps each to ride on the trail ride, they sure help if it turns cold. They both said, yes, and they liked the style of my chaps. We all decided we should leave about 7:30 a.m. in the morning. They left and said, see you in the morning.

I got on the phone and called Big "T" Trailers in Mesquite. I told him who I was and I might need another 14-foot trailer and some more axles for carts and wagons. He told me he had two 14-foot trailers with primer coat, ready for any color I wanted. I said I would get back with him. Tuesday morning, Mr. Brady and his grandsons drove up about 8 a.m. I said he could follow Pam and me that we would go to Joe's saddle shop first and look at chaps. Joe had one pair of tan chaps ready and he could make another pair and have them ready in a few days. I said that would be fine. I told Joe to make the letters "BB" and "WB" and sew them on the chaps at the bottom of each leg. Joe said, okay. I told Billy and Willy this would be a way to prove the chaps belong to them. Then we went to a western store. I picked 5 pair of Wrangler jeans and shirts. Then we picked out the boots for them to wear. Then I picked 2 Wrangler jackets for them. Then we went to dinner. After dinner, we went back to our place. We saddled the horses and rode around. I gave them pointers on how to ride. Then Mr. Brady wanted to pay us for everything, including the trailer. I figured up everything and Mr. Brady wrote me a check. I told him to make the check out to Circle W Enterprise. I asked Mr. Brady if they all wanted to ride with us to the Beaumont sale barn. They looked at each other and said, yes, what time to be here. I told them to be here about 7:30 a.m. They said, okay, and asked what we were going to do tomorrow, Wednesday. I told them we would be in Kirbyville. We both worked at the sale barn on Wednesday.

Mr. Brady wanted to know if we were going on the salt grass trail ride. I told him we would be in Houston at the rodeo, but not on the trail ride. He looked me and asked why. Well, Pam and I would be competing in the rodeo. I would ride in the saddle bronc riding and steer wrestling, and Pam would haze for me and compete in barrel racing. They all looked surprised, then asked how long had I been competing in rodeos. Well, about four years now, I will look for you all at the rodeo you all get to ride in the Grand Entry. They said, great! I told them to go ahead and ride their horses tomorrow, and we will see you all Friday. After they left, Pam and I drove to Kirbyville. I told Porter about what all had been going on. We worked the sale and went back to Nederland that evening. Thursday we worked the gray dogging team, Salty and Steeler. Friday, the Brady's showed up. We all started saddling horses. I turned and asked Mr. Brady if he wanted to ride along. He said, no, his back couldn't take it anymore. Then I told him about the two-wheel cart we had. It would be like sitting in a pickup. Mr. Brady looked at the cart and said he would give it a try. I caught one of the gray 53" ponies and put a black harness on him, then hooked him to one of the carts. Mr. Brady said it felt good. Willy and Billy rode to their horses. Pam and I rode Salty and Steeler. Every time I looked at Mr. Brady he was smiling. When we got back, Mr. Brady said he never thought he'd ever get work with horses any more. Then he asked if I would sell the complete rig, and how much. I said, sure, and the complete rig is $600. I also have another complete rig that I would sell. Then I showed him the other cart and another gray horse like the one he wants. Mr. Brady said he had a brother that lives next door and I'll bet he will want it. Then I asked where he lived and what he did for a living. Mr. Brady said he and his brother are rice farmers. He lives out past Port Acres, take Highway 365, cross Hildebrandt Bayou, then go a couple of miles, turn right on the first road, cross the Bayou again and go about two miles. You will see two houses on the left. The first house is my brother's, and we live next door and I know the roads well.

He wanted to know how he could haul three horses and a cart. I told him it was easy, he could take the shafts off the cart, just pull the pins. Put the cart in the pickup and the three horses in the trailer. He said that would work. Then he could bring his brother tomorrow to look at the other horse and cart. I said, sure. The next day they all showed up. His brother looked at the rig and I showed him how to hook it all up. He wrote me a check, they loaded up the cart and horse, and they left. Monday, I called Big "T" Trailers. Mr. T answered the phone. I told him who I was and I told him I sold my 14-foot stock trailer, and asked if he had any more. Mr. T said he had two in stock, with a primer coat and could paint it any color. I told him to paint the trailer the same tan he had painted my rodeo trailer. Then I asked if he had any axles like the ones I got before. Mr. T asked how many I needed, and said he could get them. I told him four axles with Ford spindles and he said he could deliver at the Kirbyville auction barn. I told him Thursday would be fine. I would give the driver a check for the trailer and four axles.

Monday evening a fellow called me on the phone. He asked if I was the fellow that bought the 50 acres from his brother, which he had 50 acres adjoining on the north side and he would like to sell it if I was interested. I told him I might be, how much was he asking? He said $60 an acre (that would be $3000 for all) and he also has steel posts set in concrete on the corners. I told him I could meet him at the place on Highway 87 about 9 a.m., and to bring the title to the land. He said, okay, he would see me in the morning. Tuesday morning, Pam and I drove to the land on 87 Highway. We both got there about the same time. I introduced us to him and asked if all the mineral rights went with the land. He said, yes, then showed us the pipe corner marker and said it goes back the same as the other tract. I said okay, let's go to the courthouse in Newton and make the transfer. We got to the courthouse and got the paperwork done in about 30 minutes. I wrote him a check for the land and had them make me a copy. Then we went to the bank and I put the title in the safety deposit box I had rented and put the copy in my briefcase. Then we drove out to Uncle Jud's and visited with them and told them we had bought another 50 acres next to the other. Uncle Jud smiled and said I hope you know what you are doing, that land isn't anything but a rock pile.

After dinner, Pam and I drove to the sale barn and booked cows that came early. We spent the night in the cabin at the sale barn, and the next night also. Thursday morning about 7 a.m., the truck arrived with our 14-foot stock trailer. The 4-foot axles were inside. I wrote the check for the stock trailer and the four axles, put the check in an envelope, and gave it to the driver. We hooked the trailer to the pickup and headed home. Pam and I kept on working the pair of gray horses and also another pair as well. Christmas came and went and we kept on working at the sale barn and the pair of gray horses. Pam and I were starting to think Fort Worth Rodeo. We started getting ready, packing clothes, checking saddles, and everything. We were thinking what kind of year 1948 had been and what 1949 would be – oh well, time will tell.

CHAPTER 10
1949

WE DIDN'T TRY TO MAKE THE Denver rodeo as it was too far and too cold. The Fort Worth rodeo was to start January 24th, so a bunch of us started getting ready to leave on Tuesday, the 21st, so we could get a good place to set up. Porter said he would not try to go since he had to operate the sale barn. Toby and Cody LeBlanc called, and I asked them to drive over on Monday, the 20th, and told them how to get here. Herb and Dot led the way, Pam and I were next, then Joe, and Toby and Cody LeBlanc, and Dub, the horseshoer was last. We got to the Will Rogers Coliseum about 2:30 p.m. Norm and Homer were there waiting at the gate. He had told the gate man about us. Homer had windshield stickers for all of us. Norm led us to a big building that had stalls to keep our horses in. We all set up like we had done before.

Pam and I entered our usual events, but I did not enter the bareback event. I never saw so many cowboys at one rodeo. There was one group of brothers that came the next day and set up close by. They were the Frymons from Limon, Colorado. There were four brothers and their wives. Their wives were all barrel racers and the brothers were calf ropers, steer wrestlers, or bull riders. One of them was Doug Frymon, and Herb knew him and walked over and was talking to them. They unloaded a nice sorrel horse with a white mane and tail. The horse was a little over 14 hands high. Herb and Doug was looking at the horse, he was a roping and barrel racing horse. Herb brought Doug and his wife over to us and introduced us to them. Before the rodeo was over, we knew all of the Frymons. They were also going to the Houston Rodeo next. I also mounted Doug on my dogging team and he made money on my dogging team and with another brother. There were about five top saddle bronc riders there and maybe five or six top broncs. The only way I could place was if they did not all draw those top horses. I did place two times, but it was one fifth and one sixth. I watched the entire doggers real close. They would turn their steer and throw him when the steer was still moving. I started trying this and I improved my dogging a lot.

About four days before the rodeo was over, I saw Herb and Doug looking at Doug's sorrel horse. Herb waved at me to come over. The horse was holding his left front leg up. When he walked, his leg would not straighten out. Doug asked if I knew what was wrong. He said that Herb told him I knew a lot about horse injury. I looked at his hoof, the sole seemed ok. Then I felt his knee and it was a little warm. I told Doug that I had seen this before or something close. I told Doug I thought it was a sprained knee. It may take a month or maybe three months to get well. It's like when a person twists an ankle, it depends how bad it is. I told him to take him home and put him in a lot and let him rest. Doug asked what was he going to do; his wife was up in the barrel racing tomorrow. Pam looked at me and I nodded my head. Pam told him his wife could use Steeler if she wanted. Doug looked surprised. Herb joined in and said he had seen us do that before. Doug thanked us and took his horse and put him in his stall. When the rodeo was over, I had done pretty well. I had won $450 on the two broncs I had. I had made $1700 in the dogging, altogether. Pam had won $350 in barrel racing. Monday morning, we all said our good-byes and would see them at Houston. We got home Monday evening and unloaded the horses. We let Salty and Steeler rest; they had done well at Fort Worth.

We went to Kirbyville Tuesday. I brought Porter up to date, and we talked about going to Houston. Pam and I went to Newton, stopped at the bank, and made a deposit, then went to Uncle Jud's. Tuesday evening we went back to the sale barn to tag any cows that came in and we stayed in the cabin that night. Wednesday morning, Porter and his wife got to sale early. We were talking about getting ready to go to Houston. We were going to leave next Tuesday. I suggested to Porter that when we got all set up at Houston, instead of Mrs. Porter driving back by herself, he could leave his motor home and horses with us, I would take care of them. He could take my '47 pickup and follow her home as soon as we all got stickers on our trucks so they could get back in. Pam and I would put all our stuff in our rodeo trailer, that we would not need the pickup. He could work the sale at Kirbyville and drive back Thursday since the rodeo started Friday. Mrs. Porter could drive to Houston with Mike and Jeff on Friday. (She got an O.K. from the school for Mike and Jeff to miss school and go to Houston.) We would ask the rodeo secretary to not have Porter up in the calf roping or dogging on Wednesdays the whole rodeo. Porter and his wife both liked the idea of her not driving back by herself. They said ok, and they would meet us Tuesday morning at the Beaumont sale barn. We worked the sale and came home Wednesday evening. Dub and Joe were both at the sale. They wanted to come to our place Monday evening so we could leave together. Herb said he and Dot would meet us at the sale barn or at the café.

The LeBlanc brothers from Louisiana called and I asked them to come to our place on Monday. Joe and Dub was going to be here and we would all go to the café Tuesday morning. They said, fine, they would see us Monday evening. Monday, everyone showed up and set up camp. Tuesday morning, we all left early and went to have breakfast at the café next to the sale barn. After breakfast we all headed to Houston. At Houston, Homer and Norm were waiting for us with windshield stickers. We set up and I unhooked my trailer and blocked it up so it didn't move. We all got stalls and locked them. Porter took our '47 pickup and followed Mrs. Porter back home. The Frymon brothers drove up and parked next to us. Doug and his wife were traveling with one of his brothers. His brother had a one-ton box van truck that they all stayed in. Two other brothers parked next to them. They only had three horses and one-barrel horse and one dogging horse. Doug told us his sorrel horse is still limping and he had to leave him at home. I told Doug it might take two or three months for the horse to get well. Doug asked if I would mount him in the dogging and maybe his wife in the barrel racing. I told him, sure, we could tell the secretary and they would work it so not too many would be up on the same show. We all help each other in their events they're competing in. Doug and his wife did well with their horses.

Friday, before the rodeo was over on Sunday, I noticed Doug looking at Porter's motor home and trailer. Then he asked Porter if he would sell his complete rig and Porter said he would sell the truck and two-horse trailer, but not the horses. Then Doug asked if I would sell my dogging team. I told Doug that, I would sell the horses, but not the rodeo trailer. Then Porter asked how he would get his horses home. I told him he could use my rodeo trailer that it looked like I would not need it. Porter and Doug made their deal, and then Doug asked how much for my team. I told him $4000 each horse and $150 for each saddle and bridle. Doug said ok, if I would take a check, though he could pay some cash. I told him that a check and cash was ok. Doug told me their plan was to go to the San Antonio Livestock Show and Rodeo, then to the El Paso Rodeo, then to Scottsdale, Arizona, Albuquerque, New Mexico, Colorado Springs, the Cheyenne Frontier Days, the Pendleton Roundup, then on to Walla Walla and then to Calgary. I said you sure got a big schedule ahead of you. You will probably make your money back by Cheyenne. He said he sure hoped so.

Monday morning we hooked my rodeo trailer to Porter's ranch wagon and loaded Dapple and Smokey. Doug loaded Salty and Steeler and headed for San Antonio. We all got in line and headed home. I told Porter I would pick up my trailer in the morning and he said ok. When we got to Beaumont, everyone went their own way. We got home and I brought my folks up to date. Tuesday morning, we stopped by Porter's and got our rodeo trailer. Porter thanked us again for all we did. We both said we didn't mind at all. We were on our way to the bank in Newton and then on to Uncle Jud's, and then back to the sale barn this evening and tag what livestock came in. Wednesday, Porter asked us to come to the office, that he wanted me to call Big "T" Trailers at Mesquite about a four-horse trailer. I called Big "T" and told him who I was and that I was calling for a friend of mine. Mr. T was glad to hear from me. He asked what he would pull the trailer with, and if he wanted a bumper pull or a gooseneck pull. Porter said he wanted a gooseneck pull. He was going to buy a new one-ton truck. Mr. T asked if Porter wanted a print out with different styles. Porter said, yes, he would like that and put the prices on them. Mr. T said he would put it in the mail today.

We worked the sale and talked to Uncle Jud about corn planting. We decided we would start Friday planting corn and maybe Saturday. We would go home this evening (Wednesday) and come back Friday a.m. Thursday, we went to the grocery store and bought a bunch of things to help out and that evening we decided to go on to Newton. We got an early start Friday. Pam hooked up the red donkeys to the two-wheel cart with the disk behind. I hooked up the gray donkey, Pete, and the line back dun also (Buck) and we went on disking while Uncle Jud got the corn planter ready. He hooked Big Red and Rusty to a two-wheel cart with the planter behind it. When I saw him coming, I got in front of him and set the disk to make a row. We planted while Pam kept disking. We worked till noon and went to the barn and let the stock rest. About 2:30, we all went back and planted some more. Saturday, we planted some more. Uncle Jud said, let's stop for now. He wanted to space the crop out, so we could have fresh corn all along.

Saturday evening we came home and saw that Harry and Arlene had another two-wheel cart about half built. We visited Saturday evening and we all went for a ride. We rode the next pair of rodeo horses, Grey Eagle and Grey Hawk. Sunday evening, Ed Brown called. He had a fellow that wanted to look at the gravel and sand on Highway 87 and asked if I could I meet a company field man Monday morning. I told him we would be at the property on Highway 87 about 10 a.m. Monday. Ed said that would be fine, he would tell the man 10 a.m. Monday. I thanked Ed and said we would stop by his office on the way. Monday, Pam and I got up early. We loaded Grey boy and Star since they needed to be ridden some. We stopped at the café next to the Beaumont sale barn and ate breakfast. We got to Ed Brown's office between Kirbyville and Bleakwood. His office is in his house as he had not built his new home yet. We got there about 9 a.m. and drove around to the back. I asked Ed if we could leave our truck and trailer here that we wanted to ride our saddle mules. Ed said, sure and I asked if he would look at the sand and gravel sale before we signed anything. Ed said, sure, he would be glad to and his wife is a notary and could authorize it.

We unloaded Grey boy and Star, put our chaps on, and headed for the property on 87. I got two can drinks out of the cooler to drink on the way. We got there at 9:55 a.m. and noticed a car on the side of the road and I told Pam that I bet that is the man up ahead. We finished our drinks and put the empty cans in our saddlebags. I rode up to the car and asked if he was broke down and offered to help him. He answered right quick saying, no we could not. He was here to meet a big shot and he did not need the likes of us hanging around, for us to just go on and do our thing, unless we know the president of Circle W Enterprise. Pam said, "I know who you are talking about." (I said to myself, "Well, here we go again".) Let me see if I can reach him. She reached in her saddlebag and got her drink can. I reached and got my can from my saddlebag, I had ridden about twenty feet by then. Pam held the can to her mouth and said, "Breaker. Breaker. Come in Circle W." By then I had my can at my mouth. "This is the Circle W, do you read me?" Pam came right back and said, "I read you loud and clear. I have the Field Rep here and he wants to know how far you are away, that he is tired of waiting." I said, "Tell him I am real close and I don't want to keep a big shot waiting." The Field Rep got out of his car and said, "You kids are playing a trick on me and I am here to see the president of Circle W." Pam said "Well, you are looking at the president and the vice-president. If you don't want to believe it, that is your problem." I rode back up to his car and asked if he was ready to do business or did he want to get his boss, Mr. Ben Bradley, the president of East Texas Sand and Gravel at Jasper, Texas. I have his phone number right here. His face turned red and he threw a double barrel fit sideways! We sat there on our mules, grinning at him. When he slowed down, I told him when we rode up on our mules that we had offered to help if he was broke down. Now, we don't want to do business with you at all.

Pam and I turned our mules and headed toward Ed Brown's office. When we got to Ed Brown's office, I told him word-for-word what happened. Ed and his wife went to laughing. Ed said he would give anything to have been there. Ed asked if we would like for him to call Ben Bradley, they were good friends and he thought we could still make the deal. I told Ed that would be fine with me. I don't think I want to do business with Mr. Grumpy. Ed called his friend, Ben Bradley. Mr. Bradley apologized for letting the wrong person go on a business deal like this. The man's mother and Mr. Bradley's wife are cousins. Mr. Bradley was going to give him a promotion to fencerow cleaner. He wanted to know if he could meet us at one p.m., that he is very much interested in closing the deal on the sand and gravel. We both said that would be fine. Ed Brown asked us to make a list of what all we wanted and he would act as our agent at no charge. Well, I told Ed, we were only selling sand, gravel, and clay no water rights, no timber, no coal, or minerals. We wanted a 200-foot clearance around the property and not to go within 300 feet of the creek and nothing on the other side of the creek. Ed thought we had made good sense on what we had asked. We ate dinner with Ed and his wife.

Mr. Bradley drove up at 12:55 p.m. and we all shook hands and he asked if he could take pictures of Pam and me on our mules. We both put our chaps on and Mr. Bradley took about four pictures, and then asked if Ed would take pictures of all of us standing in front of our mules. Ed asked Ben to make us all copies of the pictures, also, to go by the Ford dealership in Jasper and show the salesman the pictures. Then Ed told him about Pam and I trying to buy a truck from him, and everything the salesman said. Then he told him about the Ford dealership in Kirbyville and how we had him call Jasper and tell him we paid cash for a truck. Mr. Bradley laughed and said he would like to have been there and seen it all happen. He will go by there when the pictures are back and show them. Then we all went to the land on Highway 87. Pam and I rode our mules. Ed and Mr. Bradley followed us in Mr. Bradley's pickup. I had already told Ed that I thought we should get $50 and acre-foot. (Digging down ten feet would be $500, and so on.) Also, we wanted a check monthly. Ed worked as an agent and Ben Bradley agreed to what we asked. Then I asked how long before they would start hauling. Ben said that it would probably be 2-3 months. They would start taking bids on an eight-foot chain link fence around what they were going to haul from. They would start with rubber tire front-end loaders, and later bring in a dragline to dig deep with. They had to line up truckers to haul on a load basis. Then I asked how long would they haul from this place. Ben said they might be as long as five years. Also, any fencing is to stay when they are through.

Ed and Ben drove on back to Ed's office. Ben had all the papers with him and by the time Pam and I got there, the papers were ready. Pam and I read the papers and everything was like we wanted. We signed the papers and Mrs. Brown notarized it. Ben Bradley was pleased with the deal and so were we. He said it was a pleasure to do business with us. I told him the same thing and thanked Ed Brown for helping. We loaded our mules and went to Uncle Jud's farm and told him about the sand and gravel deal. He was glad for us. After dinner Monday, we planted some corn; and Tuesday morning we planted purple hull peas. Tuesday evening we rode our mules to Kirbyville and tagged stock that was brought in early. Wednesday, we worked the sale. Wednesday evening, we rode back to uncle Jud's. Thursday, we planted again and went home Thursday evening. Friday, we worked with dogging teams. (While Pam and I were closing the deal on the sand and gravel, Porter had bought a new one-ton truck and a new, gooseneck trailer to rodeo with.) We started working Grey Hawk and Grey Eagle. They were working real well. We also started working Ringo and Rambo. Rambo and Grey Eagle were making good barrel horses.

I was checking the feed we had and decided to go to Young's Feed and draw on the feed credit we had. J. Young was telling us that Pat had outgrown Bud, the kid horse that looks like a small Clydesdale. He said Pat has been barrel racing around at local rodeos using Mike's buckskin or Dean's palomino, but they're just not fast enough, and he asked if we had a good, fast barrel horse and would I still want "Bud?" I told him I would like to have Bud back, and we had two-barrel horses they need to come try out. J. said there is a high school rodeo this Saturday night right here in Nederland. I asked J. for all his family to come over Saturday after dinner, Pat can ride Bud and Mike and Dean can ride their horses. We can put barrels out and Mike and Dean can run the barrels. I have a stopwatch and we will time their horses and then time this horse, Rambo, and see how fast he is. Then Pat, Dean, and Mike can ride over from here to the rodeo. This way Pat can see if she wants Rambo or not. Then J. wanted to know how much for Rambo. I told him $1800, and I will give $300 in trade for "Bud," I will take $1000 in feed like we have done before, and a check for $500. J. said, isn't that kind of high for a horse? I said not if you are going to haul him around to rodeos. If you are going to take him home and not use him, then it is high. I can haul him to rodeos and get more than that. You let Pat take him to this Saturday rodeo, if she doesn't like him bring him back and I will get in some more horses. J. said ok, we will come over after dinner Saturday and try him. I got six 50-lb. sacks of feed on the draw I had with J. on the horses he got from me.

Saturday we set the barrels up. Pam and I walked them through the barrels a few times. After dinner, Mike, Dean, and Pat rode up on their horses. J. and his wife were in a pickup truck. Mike and Dean ran the barrels as fast as they could and we timed them. Then Pat ran the barrels and Rambo was four seconds faster. Pat was grinning and picking at Mike and Dean. I told them, let's do it again. This time Rambo was 4 ½ seconds faster. J. told me that Mike and Dean were to be the pick up persons at the rodeo. J. said why don't we saddle up and ride over to the rodeo since it is not far. I told J. we just might do that. Harry and Arlene drove up just as the Youngs were leaving. I told Harry and Arlene about the high school rodeo there in Nederland, and what they thought about going, and that we could ride from here. They liked the idea of riding to the rodeo. We ate supper then rode to the rodeo arena. J. Young and his wife drove up in the pickup. He and his wife came over to us and asked if I had a trailer that would haul three horses. It looks like his kids are going to rodeos a lot and they need a bigger trailer than his 4 x 10 trailer. I told J. I had a 5 x 14 foot trailer that will haul three horses easy. The trailer is real nice and it can be slept in if needed. He asked if they could look at the trailer on Sunday about 2 p.m. and I told him, sure. They all came and looked at the trailer and asked how much. I told him $1400. J. wrote me a check and we hooked it to his ranch wagon, and they left. Harry asked what they were going to do for a trailer. I told him he could use the 14-foot rodeo trailer, I was going to buy a new 16-foot rodeo trailer. Harry grinned and said that would work.

Monday morning I called Big "T" Trailers in Mesquite. I asked Mr. T if he had any 16-foot rodeo trailers in stock, and when could he deliver it to the sale barn in Kirbyville. Mr. T said he had one with windows on both sides and he could paint it and have it at the sale barn Thursday about 7 a.m. I asked how much. He told me $1600 for the deluxe model, what color did I want? I told him the same tan as before, and I would give the driver a check like before. Mr. T thanked me and said it was a pleasure doing business with me. Tuesday morning we left for Kirbyville sale barn. I told my folks we would not be home till Thursday. We went on to Ed Brown's office and I told him to cut the timber at the gravel land. The timber might be easier to get out before the fence is built. Ed said he would get the timber cutters right away. I told him to cut only the pine and sweet gum. He said, ok. Then he typed up a contract and I signed it. We then went back to the sale barn. We worked the sale and told Uncle Jud we would spend the night in the cabin at the sale. Next morning about 7 a.m., the new 16-foot rodeo trailer arrived. I gave the deliveryman a check and we hooked the trailer up and went home. Uncle Jud got there to clean up the pens just as we started to leave. We showed him the trailer. He liked it and said it was a lot bigger. We got home and showed my folks the trailer. Friday, Harry and Arlene came and they liked the trailer, also.

Saturday morning a man called about selling us the 47 acres that joins the land on the north on the Highway 87 property. He told me he sold the three acres to a fellow and he was going to build a house and truck farm it. When he saw all the gravel, he changed his mind. His brother bought the three acres and that is how the land ended. I told the man I would buy the land and pay him $60 an acre, like I paid for the other, when did he want to meet us. I asked about Monday morning about 8:30. He said that would be good and he would bring the title. Monday morning Pam and I met the man on the 47 acres. It had six-inch steel pipe on the corners. We then went to the courthouse in Newton and had the paperwork done. I wrote the man a check. He thanked us, and I had copies made and went to the bank, and put the original paper in our safety deposit box. I put my copy in my briefcase, and then we went on to Uncle Jud's. I told him about buying another tract adjoining the gravel hill. He asked what I was going to do with all that gravel and I told him about selling the gravel deal and the timber deal. Then he smiled and said good for you. Then we started planting. We had done well and were just about through.

Tuesday we drove the '47 pickup and stopped at Ed Brown's office. I told Ed about buying another 47 acres. He asked what I was going to tell Ben Bradley about the land. I told him that I did not care if he knew I had bought it, I am going to wait and see how the deal goes on the 100 acres. Ed smiled and thought that was a good idea. We went on to Kirbyville and worked the sale. Herb and Dot were there and we talked about the Jasper Rodeo that was going to be the next following weekend. It would start on Thursday night, continue Friday night, and then have two shows on Saturday. We would all go Thursday early and get set up. The rodeo contractor wanted to know if the lady was going to be there with her donkey. I told him to hold on, she is right here. He said to tell her he would pay her $10 a show. Her riding the donkey in the barrel racing is a good crowd draw. Arlene said to tell him they are planning to be there. I told him that and asked if he needed another pickup man. He said, yes, and asked if he is the same one as last year. I told him, yes, and would see him Thursday.

Wednesday before the rodeo, Harry and Arlene came out. We hooked up the 14-foot trailer to the '47 pickup. (It has a four-speed transmission and pulls a trailer good.) Pam and I would take the new 16-foot trailer and haul Grey Hawk and Grey Eagle and Pedro in it. We would leave early Thursday. Harry and Arlene both had to work Thursday and Friday. Pam would ride Pedro in the barrel racing on Thursday. When they got off work on Friday, they would drive out to our place, put just Bill in the trailer that is hooked to the '47 truck (leave his '46 there) and drive to Jasper. I would be the pickup man on Thursday. The newspaper had a picture with Arlene on Pedro and had a write up about a donkey running barrels. Pam rode Pedro Thursday night and the crowd really hollered. Pedro knew he was a star. The rest of the show, Arlene rode Pedro. Harry and Arlene really liked the 14-foot trailer. There are lots of cowboys sleeping in their trailers. Pam and I did well at the rodeo. I was able to build my bank account back up. Sunday morning we all went home.

The big trail ride on the Sabine River was set up for the second weekend in May. I had been talking to the same bunch, and some new ones, about going. Dad could not go this time, he was working days. I was telling Herb and Dot about it. They only had two horses and Cindy would sure want to go. I asked Herb if they could haul three horses in their trailer, that I had Ringo that he could use. I would not take Grey Hawk and Grey Eagle, they were too valuable. Herb said he would appreciate it. They would come by our place on Friday a.m. and pick up Ringo. We kept on planting and got through a week before the trail rides on Highway 87. Friday morning, Herb and family came by early. We all loaded up and left for Highway 87. Harry and Arlene would leave Friday evening when they got off work. We had a good ride, and made a lot of new friends. Friday and Saturday night, we all set around the campfire and did some picking and singing. Sunday morning we all met at the big tent and had church. We sang gospel songs, Ed did the talking. We loaded up later and all went home. Ed told us we should do this ride again.

Monday morning early, I called the Starr ranch. I had sold Pat, my barrel horse, and needed another horse. I told Bill Starr what we needed.

He asked Pam and me to leave after dinner and drive out, pick what we wanted, spend the night, and drive back Tuesday. I told him I just needed three head. He said, that was ok, that we would have a good visit. We loaded up, hooked the 16-foot trailer up and headed out. We got to Livingston and stopped at the saddle shop. He had one good, all-around saddle and one old, old saddle. He wanted $75 for the good saddle and $25 for the old one. He said the old saddle needed oiling and cleaning and checking out. He would have them ready tomorrow. I said, ok, I wanted both and would stop by about 8:30 or 9 a.m. and get them. He said that would be fine. We got to the Starr Ranch about 6 p.m. and looked at some good, gray horses. We picked a dark gray horse about 15 hands for a hazing and barrel horse. Then I told Bill I needed a couple of real gentle riding horses. Bill took us over to another pen. There was a pair of roan horses just shy of 14 hands that would work and ride. I asked, how much for the three horses. Bill said the gray horse is $300 and the roan horses are $250 each. I wrote him a check on the Circle W account. We sat around and visited till time to turn in. We loaded up next morning and headed to Livingston. I paid him for the two saddles, put them in the panel truck and headed for home. We got home right after dinner. I called Big "T" Trailers and asked about a 16-foot stock trailer. Mr. T said he had a 16-foot deluxe, stock trailer painted green. It has one open space 3 inches wide on each side for cool air, and can be closed up for winter. I asked how much and Mr. T said $900, and that he is delivering another trailer to the sale barn in Beaumont Thursday a.m. I told him I would take the trailer and give the truck driver a check like before. Pam and I went to the sale barn in Beaumont Thursday a.m. We hooked the trailer to the '47 pickup, gave the driver a check, and came home. Friday, Pam and I rode Ringo and Blue, the new horse to the Beaumont sale barn; this gave the horses a good workout.

Saturday, Harry and Arlene came out and we decided to go for a ride. Just as we got saddled up, a man and his wife drove up. They were about 45 or 50 years old. They said they lived out close to the Brady's and saw their horses and asked them about them. Mr. Brady told them about us and recommended they see what we have. I told them about a pair of roan horses, and asked them to go ride with us. That is a good way to see if you like them. They said ok if we didn't mind. I put two good saddles on the roan horses. We rode about 2 hours. They asked how much. I told them $600 with saddles. They said they would take them. Then he asked if I had a good trailer and I showed them the brand new 16-foot trailer. I told them the price was $995 and they bought the whole deal. They gave me a check for all of it. We helped them load up and they left. Monday, Pam and I rode Grey Eagle and Grey Hawk, since they needed to be ridden some. Tuesday, we loaded Grey boy and Star and headed to Newton. As we got to Ed Brown's office, the orange flag was out, so we stopped to see what he wanted. Ed wanted to tell us about a museum that is trying to take place. He told us about a grocery store in Newton that had closed down. The owner had retired and gave the building to the city. Ed and the Mayor both belong to the Lions Club and maybe the Lady Lions could run it and be a fund raiser. I told Ed we had an old doctor's buggy that came with the Adam's place. We would loan the buggy to the museum, and if the museum were a success we would later donate it to the museum. The buggy will need cleaning and maybe repairs. Ed told us the history teacher at the high school likes to restore things, maybe he would do it. When Ed told him about the buggy, the teacher said he would be glad to help. I got in touch with T.J. Adams and he was glad the buggy was going to a museum and he would like to help restore it. I asked T.J. if he would like to present the buggy to the museum since it was his granddaddy's buggy, and that he had been a country doctor that used it. He said, yes. The history teacher and T.J. got together and they started working on the buggy. They worked in their spare time and it took about a month to get it ready. While they worked spare time on the buggy, we kept working the sale barn.

One Tuesday morning we were driving along, Pam saw the orange flag out at Ed Brown's office. I knew he wanted something so we stopped and went in. Ed had us a check for the timber on Highway 87 gravel place. We thanked him and he thanked us for letting his company cut it. The gravel company had already started hauling gravel. They would haul some gravel all the way on Highway 87 past the old Salem community. That part of 87 is still a dirt road and it needs building up before they hard surface it. Each time we rode by I would notice they were hauling gravel. Eastex Gravel had bought two of the biggest rubber-tired, front-end loaders I had ever seen and they were four-wheel drive. The first thing they did was level the hill in the middle. The land was 6 acres wide and 8 acres long, each nearly 50 acres tracts. They had to leave one acre (210 x 210) from the highway and two acres from the back where the timber and creek was. They would leave five acres in the middle and they could haul gravel and sand. When they got the hill leveled up, they could tell about how deep to haul to get down to ground level. When they were done, the hill was about six feet higher than ground level. They are to pay Circle W $50 an acre-foot deep. Both 50-acre tracts would be about 25 surface acres, each tract. I figured Circle W would have about a 50-acre lake when they were through. I did not know how deep yet but I hoped it would be 25-30 foot deep. Pam said we just might do well on this gravel and sand deal. I said I sure do hope so.

We started telling everyone about driving the doctor's buggy to town and wanted lots of riders to ride with us. We would take the buggy from the Adam's place and use the donkey, Pete, to pull the buggy. Uncle Jud wanted to use the buckskin donkey and a two-wheel cart on the drive. Ed Brown and his wife wanted to use Big Red and Rusty, Uncle Jud's two mules. This ride was going to happen next Saturday. Pam and I went on Thursday. Harry and Arlene came out Friday after they got off work. Pam and I would haul Gray Boy and Star. Harry and Arlene would haul Bill and Pedro. We had the 14-foot rodeo trailer hooked to the '47 pickup. Pam and I had the new 16-foot trailer hooked to our '49 panel truck. Soon as they got here, we left for Uncle Jud's farm in Newton. We all spent the night there. Saturday morning, riders started showing up at the Adam's place. We put the harness on Pete and a saddle on Buck, the two donkeys. The history teacher who helped restore the buggy rode with T.J. We had lots of riders. We had news reporters there from Jasper and Beaumont. They took pictures all the way to town. The presentation of the buggy was a big success. After it was all over, we all went back to the Adam's place. T.J. must have thanked me three or four times for letting him present the buggy. I told him that was the way it should be.

When we got back to Uncle Jud's, Ed Brown asked Uncle Jud if he would sell him Big Red and Rusty. He said they need them to ride and check timberland. Uncle Jud came over to me and asked what I thought about selling the mules. I told him to sell them, that I could probably find another pair of donkeys, that I liked donkeys better than mules so Uncle Jud sold Ed the mules and saddles. Ed and his wife rode the mules back to his office. Pam and I and Harry and Arlene rode along with them. When we got to Ed's office, we turned around and went back to Uncle Jud's.

CHAPTER 11
July, 1949

MONDAY, HOMER AND NORM CAME OUT to our place in Nederland. The Diamond S Rodeo Company was putting on a rodeo in Beaumont next Thursday night, Friday night, Saturday afternoon, and Saturday night. They wanted to know if we would be there, they said they could use two pickup men. I told them we would, and that Harry and I could be pickup men. I would use Cody and Harry would use Bill. Homer said the Diamond S is going to Marshall, Texas the following weekend, and asked if we would go there also. I told him Pam and I would go, but didn't think Harry would go as it was too far. Homer and Norm left and said they would see us at the Beaumont Rodeo. We got our first check on the gravel. We decided to put the check in the Newton Bank as that is the county the gravel is in. I called Harry and told them about the rodeo in Beaumont. They were glad that he would make some extra money. They also wanted Arlene and Pedro to run the barrels. Pam and I went to Kirbyville to work the sale and we told everyone about the rodeo. Then we went home Wednesday after the sale to get ready.

Thursday morning we hooked the 14-foot trailer to the '47 pickup. Then we hooked the 16-foot rodeo trailer to the '49 panel truck. This way, all Harry and Arlene had to do is park the '46 pickup. We would have all the horses loaded. We worked the rodeo and went home at night. Harry and Arlene went home since they both had to work Friday. We did well at the rodeo. I made money in the dogging and the saddle bronc riding. Homer came up to Pam and I and he told us he was short two-truck drivers and asked if we could help out. Pam would drive Homer's pickup and pull the travel trailer. He could drive one truckload of rodeo stock, Norm could drive one truck, and I would drive one truck. We would leave Monday morning. Norm would pick us up and we would leave for Marshall. We said that would be ok. We figured it would take about five hours to get there. I told my folks where we were going. Norm picked us up early Monday and we went to get the trucks. Pam and I put a change of clothes in one duffle bag. Pam kept the bag with her in the pickup. We got to Marshall that afternoon. We all spent the night in the travel trailer. Norm took us to the bus station. We had to go home and get ready to go back to Marshall for the rodeo. I got our duffle bag and told Norm we'd see him Wednesday that we would all leave from Kirbyville after the sale. The bus left out, and I think the bus stopped at every little town. About 10 a.m., when we were about five miles north of Jasper, the bus broke down just as we got to a crossroad. There was a small café on the right side of the road. All the passengers went to the café. The bus driver called in trying to get help.

Pam and I saw a general store across the dirt road on the same side of the highway. We looked just back of the store and there was a pen with two big, gray donkeys in it. We went over to the donkeys and they came up to us to be petted. One donkey was a little lighter than the other. The light one went to Pam and the darker one came to me. They both had a stripe down their back with a shoulder stripe. They were about 53" and 54" high. We then went inside the store to ask about the donkeys. The man told us a fellow who used to live down the dirt road owned the donkeys. He had to move to Beaumont and live next to his son and he asked me to sell the donkeys for him. He said he wanted two hundred for both of them. The donkeys would work or ride, and two saddles and two sets of collars and reins go with them. I told him I didn't think the donkeys would bring that much but he wanted to get what he could. We looked at the saddles and they could definitely use some oil. We saddled up the donkeys and rode around in the pen. I told the man we would take them, and I asked if we could leave the harness and stuff here and get them later and he said sure, he would put them in the back and put my name on them. If I wanted, I could write a check and mail it to the man in Beaumont and I could put a note in the letter telling him who we are and that we would give the donkeys a good home. He had raised the donkeys and one donkey was two weeks older than the other. They were now five years old. He would always ride one and lead the other, and ride here to get supplies.

I wrote a check to the man and put a note in with the check and put the check in a mailbox outside the door.

He asked who I was, said he thought he knew me. I told him I worked at the sale barn in Kirbyville. I was a bid starter and my wife worked in the office. The bus had broke down and we didn't know how long before they could get help. We were going to ride the donkeys to Kirbyville, work the sale, and take them to my uncle's farm in Newton. I asked him how far to Jasper and he told us about five miles and then twenty miles to Kirbyville. We should make it in about five hours. We went back to the bus and got our duffle bag, then went back to the donkeys and saddled up. The man told us if he went to the sale, he would bring the harness and stuff. I told him, if we were not there to leave it with Porter. He said, ok and we headed to Jasper. We gave the donkeys a loose rein and our surprise, the donkeys both hit a single-foot gait and we had a smooth ride and made good time. We got to Kirbyville in about four hours. We put the donkeys in the same pen that we put Star and Gray Boy. Joe and Dub was already there. We were all going to the Marshall rodeo the next day. We were talking to Joe and I told him I was going to call my folks to come get us. I had to bring Cody and Toby, our dogging horses, here to Marshall. Joe spoke up and said he would take us to Nederland and drive back here and that Dub would look after Jet. He could drive it in about three hours and I told him we would sure appreciate it. We would spend the night would see them in the morning. We unhooked the trailer Dub tied Jet to a tree and Joe then took us to Nederland. We got up early in the morning and loaded our horses and drove to Kirbyville .I had told my folks we were going to Marshall. We got to Kirbyville and Uncle Jud was already there. I showed him the gray donkeys and he said they looked good. We now had three teams of donkeys. I told him I was going to unload the horses and take donkeys to the farm. He asked us to bring Aunt Willie back to help in the office. When we got there all the donkeys were braying. We put them all together and they acted like they knew each other. Pam went and got Aunt Willie and we headed to sale barn. When we got back Herb and Dot and Cindy were there. Porter came over and he told us to go ahead and leave, we had a long trip to make. Cindy got in the truck with Joe. We got in front, Joe and Cindy were next, then Herb and Dot and Dub was last. Porter was not going because he had to run the sale barn. We all traveled together. When we got back from Marshall and Uncle Jud was talking to us, I suggested he take the red pair of donkeys to use since he had red Mules. Uncle Jud liked that idea. Pam said she wanted the gaited donkeys and I could use Pete and Buck to farm with. I told Uncle Jud about the harness and tack and that the fellow would bring it all to the sale barn. Monday morning.

Pam and I then went to Nederland and unloaded the dogging team. Tuesday we drove to Kirbyville and worked the sale on Wednesday. The fellow bought the gaited donkeys and the harness and tack. We had a nice visit. I told him we made the trip with the donkeys in about four hours. He was glad the donkeys had a good home. Friday evening Harry and Arlene came out. They wanted to go to Uncle Jud's and go ride in the woods. I said good, that we would show them the pair of donkeys. We could ride Pete and Buck. We left out early Saturday. We saddled the donkeys and rode towards the Adams place. We crossed the creek and stopped at the slew just past creek. I told Harry I wanted to show them something. This is where the slew starts and goes almost to the Jasper – Newton highway 190. It looks like the highway filled in the slew because the slew starts up again on the other side. I got off the donkey and started moving some sticks and limbs. In a little while we could see what looked the end of a dugout. The Caddo Indians made these dugouts out of cypress trees. Harry helped move some of the limbs. He was curious to see what it could be. The dugout had about 4 or 5 feet sticking out of the water. The rest was under water. Harry and I tried to move the dugout but it was solid as a rock. We rode back to Uncle Jud's and told him what we had found. He was really interested to see it. He wanted to go right then. We hooked up the donkeys to a two-wheel cart and Uncle Jud and Aunt Willie got on the cart. We all went back to the slew. Uncle Jud looked at the dugout and said the dugout could be twenty feet or longer. He said it was going to take a bunch of us to get it out. He thought it could be over a hundred years old.

We all went back to Uncle Jud's and after dinner we drove to Ed Brown's office. Ed was real excited. He wanted to bring his mules and he and his wife and all of us to ride to the slew. I told him ok and to be at Uncle Jud's at 1 p.m. with their mules. All of us rode back to the dugout. We knew it would be hard to get the dugout out of the slew. As we rode back, I looked at Ed and I could tell he was thinking about the dugout. When we got to Uncle Jud's, Ed suggested we try to get some of the Caddo Indians that live on the Sabine River there on the land that the Sabine River Enterprise had bought. Maybe we could all ride in to the place where the Caddos lived. (Ed and the chief had become good friends.) They might want to help get the dugout out of the slew. Ed asked if we could ride to the village next Saturday. We had to ride mules since there is not a road into the village. We could park where we parked for the trail ride. There should only be the six of us. He does not like a bunch of people coming into the village. The next Saturday we all trailered our mules to Parker's store in Bleakwood. Harry and Arlene went with us to Uncle Jud's Friday evening. We pulled the 16-foot trailer with the four donkeys. Ed and his wife were at Parker's store. We all drove to the Sabine River as close as we could. At that point we all saddled up and rode to the Caddo village. Ed told the chief about the dugout. Then he asked the chief if they wanted to help get it out of the bog. Ed told him he would send the big stock trailer after them and put bales of hay for them to sit on. He wanted the chief to be there because the chief would know if it were a Caddo dugout or not. Ed told him there would be a trailer next Saturday about 7 a.m. The chief said he would like to help and would bring lots of help. Ed told them we would see them at the Adams place next Saturday morning. We rode back to the trailers and Ed asked if it would be okay to ask the history teacher to come along since he liked things like this. I told sure and to bring help also. We got back to Uncle Jud's and told him about getting the dugout out of the slew and that we would be here next Friday evening. Jud said he would cut some four-foot sweet gum logs to help get the dugout to the creek. We would put the logs under the dugout and roll it to the creek to clean it out. We could take each end out of the ten-foot wagon, put the dugout on the wagon and the donkeys could pull it to his barn. He was sure it will need lots of work. We all thought that would be the thing to do. Saturday evening we went back to Nederland and Ed had called the history teacher and told him about the dugout. The teacher asked about asking an archeology man in Dallas about it. Ed told him sure. I had told Ed to handle it all. We went to the sale Wednesday morning and told Porter all about the dugout. Ed drove up and told us the news is out about dugout find. People from the newspaper had found out and they plan to be there for the whole thing. Ed said I might need to come up Friday morning. I told him we would be there. We would go home after the sale and be back Friday morning. Thursday I told my folks all about it and to drive up if they wanted. I called Harry and told him we had to go Friday morning and for them to drive up Friday when they got off work. He said okay they would be up.

Friday morning we drove to Ed Brown's office. He said this discovery had people calling him asking about it. He told them the Circle W owned the land and he was just helping and that the owner would be here Saturday morning. Saturday morning Ed sent Layne Hill with the gooseneck stock trailer to the pick up the Caddo chief. The chief was dressed in full Indian clothes. He had about fifteen or so young Caddos to help. Uncle Jud had cut 10 or 12 poles to help work the dugout out of the mud. There must have been a hundred or more pictures taken, some with Pam and I and the chief. The chief and I got to visit some. He was friendlier when he found out that I was part Cherokee and Pam was part Choctaw. Some of the Caddos got in the slew and worked on the dugout. We had all kinds of people giving advice but none would get in the mud and help. By noon we had the dugout about half out. The young Caddos would feel around inside the dugout. They first found an old cypress paddle. Then they felt around and found two clay pots. I thought the archeology man was going to have a heart attack when they found the pots. They took the pots to the creek and washed them out. They also found some clay pot pieces. The chief stayed close to me and we talked some. The archeology man asked if he could take a broken piece of clay back to Dallas. They wanted to try to estimate how old the pots were. I told him okay but to get the piece back. We got the dugout out of the slew about 3 p.m. We put some of the four-foot logs under the dugout and finally got to the creek. They took buckets and poured water in the dugout and cleaned it out. Then we all got around it and got it on the ten-foot wagon with both ends sticking out of the wagon. We hooked the wagon to the cart took it to Uncle Jud's barn. The history man and Uncle Jud were going to clean it out better. It may take months to get it in good shape. Ed and I were talking with Chief Joe and asked him what he thought about Ed and me dedicating it to the museum in Newton when it was cleaned. This way it could be for everyone to enjoy. Chief Joe said he would like that. I told him we would let him know when. Layne loaded all the Caddos in the stock trailer and took them back to the village on the Sabine River. We all loaded up and went home.

The next Tuesday Pam and I went to the Kirbyville sale and tagged a few cows. Wednesday Joe and Cindy drove up and told us they were engaged. We both asked if the had a date planned. They said no but they would let us know. Harry and I worked on the belly drop four-wheel wagon type trailer. It had a funnel type sides with a trap door bottom. It would open up as much as needed. Uncle Jud would use it to haul manure from the sale barn and haul it to the cornfield and unload as the donkeys pull it along. This will save unloading by hand. We got it finished in September. Pam and I started riding in August getting Gray Eagle and Grey Hawk ready to go to the Alexandria rodeo, then to the Texarkana rodeo. We rode every Friday and Monday. I rode Gray Boy and Pam rode Star, our gaited mules. I would lead Hawk, the dogging horse, and would lead Eagle the hazing and barrel horse. We would give Gray Boy and Star a loose rein and they would hit a single foot, then Hawk and Eagle would have to trot to keep up. By the time we were to go to the Alexandria rodeo the first part of September, Hawk and Eagle were in good shape. All of us went to Alexander in September. There were not a lot of bareback riders there, so I entered the bareback, saddle bronc and steer dogging. We made money in all the events. We came home Sunday after the rodeo and started getting ready to go to the Texarkana Rodeo.

Joe and Cindy and Pam and I were talking, and Joe said he and Cindy were thinking about getting married on Monday. This way they could go to Texarkana as a married couple. Also they would like to get married at our barn and on their horses Jet and Snip, and asked if my dad could marry them like he did for us. I told him I was sure Dad would marry them since he is off work until Wednesday. They could go to the courthouse and get their marriage license. We got home Sunday evening and I asked Dad about marrying Joe and Cindy and he agreed. Monday Joe and Cindy and Herb and Dot, also Cindy and Dot's dad, Doc Kase, got all the horses saddled. Doc drove a two-wheel cart with Cindy with him. They rode up to the barn from the east. Dot met Cindy with her horse Snip. Herb and Joe rode in from the west. Pam and I were riding our mules Gray Boy and Star. Dad and Mother were waiting in the hall of the barn. Dad married Joe and Cindy and they left on their honeymoon.

Tuesday morning we all loaded up and drove to Texarkana. The rodeo started on September 7th on a Friday and ended Sunday September 15th. I entered the bareback, saddle bronc, and steer dogging. Pam rode Eagle in the barrel racing and hazed for me in the dogging. We both made money in all events. One cowboy did not make any money and wanted to sell his chaps for ten dollars. So I bought them from him and then we all came home on Monday. We **had about two weeks rest before going to Dallas for the month of rodeoing in October. Monday night I called Starr ranch. I needed to get the two black mules. Bill Starr told me the mules were ready and I asked him if they had a horse that would make a barrel horse. He said he thought so as he had just traded some mares for some geldings. I told him we would be there about three or four in the afternoon, to look at the horses and would come back Wednesday. Bill said that would be fine. Tuesday morning we hooked the 16-foot stock trailer to the '49 panel truck, since it would haul four horses. We got there about three in the afternoon and Bill showed us the mules and some good horses. One horse was a sorrel that was very fast named Streak and was over fifteen hands tall. Streak was a horse that we could train to run barrels. We would take him to Dallas for the month long rodeo in October. We always need a gentle riding horse so we picked a sorrel horse about fourteen hands, kid gentle and would work and ride. This made four head. We put the mules in one pen and the sorrels in another. I wrote the Starr ranch a check on the Circle W account. We sat around visited, and I told Bill some of the things that had been happening. We spent the night and left the next morning. We stopped in Livingston at the saddle shop. We bought two saddles. One would make a good barrel saddle, and the other is just a good riding saddle. The good riding saddle had a sixteen-inch tree and adjustable stirrups. We started training Streak next morning and went to Newton that evening.

I asked Uncle Jud how he liked the belly drop manure wagon. I thought we would take the old wagon home and put a new cypress lumber bed on it. The old bed on the wagon could never get clean enough to haul corn. Uncle Jud thought it would be good to put a new bed on the wagon. He suggested we spend the night and take the wagon home Friday. I told him okay. Then I told him about going to the Starr ranch and the sorrel horse that was about fourteen hands, he looked like Big Jim only smaller. I also told him about the 4x10 horse trailer I took in trade. Uncle Jud wanted us to bring Little Jim and the trailer to Newton so he could ride him hunting. I told him okay, and I had a good sixteen-inch saddle and I would bring it too. We brought the old manure wagon home to put a new bed on it. We started working with Streak, the new barrel horse, and rode to the fresh water canal. It was about seven miles one-way. Friday, Harry and Arlene came out. I brought them up to date on all that had been happening and they spent the night. I called the Walkers and told them I had two black mules for them. They said they would be there for them in the morning. Saturday, while we were waiting for the Walkers, we took the bed off the manure wagon and made an onion bed out of it. Harry made two metal sawhorses to put the wagon bed on. When the Walkers drove up they liked the mules and said they would soon be hauled to Colorado. They wrote me a check for the mules and left. We set the wagon bed over by the first stall east of barn. We mixed dirt and manure and a good onion bed. We all went to Young's feed store and bought two bunches of multiplying onions. We came back and set the onions out in the wagon bed.

Monday, Pam and I worked Streak on the barrels and rode Eagle and Hawk. Tuesday morning we loaded Little Jim in the 4x10 horse trailer and took him to Uncle Jud's. He was happy to have a horse to ride and hunt on. We took the sixteen-inch saddle I bought in Livingston for Uncle Jud to use on Little Jim. We worked the sale Wednesday and came home that evening. We kept working Streak and we could see he was turning into a good barrel horse. Saturday Harry and Arlene came out. In a little while the whole bunch showed up. The LeBlanc brothers from southern Louisiana drove up. They had sold their dogging team and trailer. They wanted to buy Hawk and Eagle and go with us to Dallas and they also needed a trailer. I told them I would sell them Hawk and Eagle, and the sixteen foot stock trailer. I told them the pair would be $4000.00 each and $1000.00 for the 16 foot deluxe stock trailer. They said okay, that is what they sold their team for and they also wanted the trailer. They priced their team high thinking the man would not pay that much. He just said okay and wrote them a check.

The LeBlanc brothers ask to leave the trailer and horses with us. They would go home and return Monday evening. I told them that would be fine; we could travel together to Dallas. They wrote me a check and said go ahead and deposit it, that they would be back Monday evening. Pam asked what we were going to do for a dogging team. I told her we could use Cody and Toby for a dogging team and use Streak on barrels. Everybody went home and said they would be back Tuesday morning. I called Tom Smith and asked him if he had some young steers that needed to be run and to practice on. Tom told me that he had six steers he thought would be good dogging steers and he would bring them Tuesday morning. I told him good and see him Tuesday morning.

Sunday even Pam and I saddled Toby and Cody and jumped them out the chute a few times then we rode them to the fresh water canal and back. Monday morning, I called Herb and Dot and ask them to come out and help. Herb said they would be right over. Tom drove up and we put the steers in the chute. Pam hazed for me and Herb worked the gate. We ran all six steers and Toby and Cody did real well. We ran the steers again, and Toby and Cody did much better than before. We put the steers back in the trailer and took Tom back to his place. That evening the LeBlanc brothers drove up. They slept in the 16 foot trailer that night just like they would at Dallas. Tuesday morning we loaded Streak, the barrel horse, and Toby and Cody, the dogging team. The LeBlanc brothers loaded they're dogging' team as well. Soon everybody showed up and we all headed to Dallas. We got to Dallas about four p.m. Homer and Norm were waiting for us. They showed us where to park. We all put locks on the stalls we would be using for all of October. The cowboy that I bought the chaps from at Texarkana was there. He asked if he could buy back the chaps I had bought from him. I told sure and went to our trailer and got the chaps. He asked how much and I told him $10 just what I paid for them. He thanked me a couple of times, he turned out to be a nice friend, but he had just had some bad luck. He helped out with the stock that I drew and steers also. I could see Big T trailers on display from where we were set up. Pam and I walked over and talked to him. He was really glad to see us. I told him we would see him later on the last part of October because we would need some more trailers. Mr. T. said that would be good.

I mounted five to six doggers in the month of October. Pam and I together made over $3500.00. Before we left Pam and I walked over to the Big T trailer set up. We ordered two trailers, one 5x16 deluxe stock trailer and one 5x16 deluxe rodeo trailer. Mr. T. said the trailer would be delivered in about a week. I told him would be good and to paint both trailers silver. The middle of November on a Friday morning a big car drove up to our double driveway. A man got out all dressed up. I could tell he was no horseman. I told him to get out and come on over to the shed by the trailers. He told us he represented a group of investors. He was here to offer to buy this place. I ask him how much his offer was. We have ten acres, a cabin, and horse training pens. He said they would pay twenty -five thousand dollars for the place. I smiled and told him that was not even close. He can go tell the investors that they will have to pay a lot more than that. He asked how much would I take. I told him I would have to think about it, but it wouldn't be cheap. He said he would go tell the investors what I had said. He did not come back. We kept on riding our horses, keeping them in shape for Fort Worth.

Christmas came and went. It was just an average holiday season. On a Monday after Christmas I needed some feed, so we went to Young's feed. We loaded twelve fifty-pound sacks of feed. I will take six sacks to Newton and keep six here at home to feed here. We went back inside to enter the twelve sacks on our trade chart. There was a fellow there talking to J., he was a sales Rep. for a knife company in Titusville, PA., and he had several boxes of knives 10 to a box. The knives were 440 stainless steel with stag handles. I was looking at the knives and listening to the man trying to get J. to buy a box of knives. If J. would buy two boxes of knives, 10 per box, he could sell them for $2.50 each. I liked the knives very much and I asked the man if he would make a better price on more knives. He yes on fifty knives and he went to his car to see how many knives he had. I asked J. if he would mind if I bought some to get a better price and he said go ahead and try for a better price. The man came back in and said he had a little over a hundred knives, 10 boxes. I asked him to make me a price on all 100 knives. He thought for a minute then said $1.50 each. I then said how about $1.20 each for a hundred. He finally said ok. He told me the blades were different lengths, some were 4 to 5 inches long and some in between. Then he told us about some other knives he had. The factory had some 440 stainless steel left over. They had made 10 bread knives with 7-inch blades. The book showed a bread knife to have a nine-inch blade. These were a special run and the blades were all seven inches long. I told him I wanted to look at them. He went to his car and brought all the knives. They all had stag handles. I bought all ten knives for $1.20 each. I bought a hundred of the knives with the 4 to 5 inch blades for $1.20 each. I told J. I would leave two boxes of knives that he and his family could each have a knife, and he could sell the other 15 and he liked that idea. I put the rest of the knives in the truck. Pam asked what I was going to do with all those knives. I told her we would give some of them to our friends. We would pick what we wanted and give Harry and Arlene each one. My folks would each get one and Uncle Jud and Aunt Willie as well. Porter and his family would each get one also. Pam thought that would be nice. We got home and I put the feed in the feed room. I took the knives in the cabin. I put the ten knives with seven-inch blades in the footlocker. Then we laid all the knives on the table and checked to see how many of each size blade we had. I told Pam to pick what she wanted. I took one of the knives with a five-inch blade. Pam picked one with a four-inch blade to use in the kitchen. I told my folks to come over and pick a knife for them selves. Dad picked a 4-¾ inch blade and Mother picked a 4-inch blade. Tuesday morning we drove to Uncle Jud's. We gave them each a knife, which they both liked. We spent the night at Uncle Jud's and Wednesday we went to the sale barn. Mike and Jeff were out of school for the holidays, so the whole Porter family was there. I asked them all to come to the office. Dub, the horse shoer was there so I told him to come also. I gave Porter and his family each a knife and also Dub. They all thanked us a couple of times. I told them I lucked into a deal and bought a bunch. In a little while Herb and Dot, and Joe and Cindy all drove up and I gave them each a knife. They were all happy to get one.

We worked the sale Wednesday and that evening we all home. Thursday we boxed all the 5-inch blade knives in boxes. Then all 4-¾ inch in boxes and so on. Then I fixed two boxes with assorted blade length and put them in the truck. Friday evening Harry and Arlene came out and I gave them each a knife of their own choosing. Saturday we worked with Streak, the new barrel horse. Sunday morning Harry and Arlene went home. Pam and I were talking we had sold all the kid gentle horses. We needed to keep gentle horses around to have for sale. I called the Starr Ranch and Bill answered the phone. I told him we needed four gentle horses that would ride and work to a two-wheel cart. Bill said he had some and asked when we would be coming out. I made sure Monday was ok and told him we would get there around 2 or 3 p.m. Bill said that would be good. I told him we would see him then. I got out the knives and picked knives for all of the Starr family and Bill's two nephews. I also picked out one for the horse wrangler and a few extra. I put the knives in the panel truck so I would have them when I went to the Starr ranch. Then I hooked up the sixteen-foot stock trailer as it would haul four horses. Just as I got finished, a car drove up. It was my sister Viola, her husband Ray, and their son Jere, who was about three years old. Ray was in the army, stationed at Fort Polk Louisiana. He was a cook in the service. We all walked over to the folk's house to see them. We sat around and visited and Ray told us he could take a discharge from the service or if he stayed in they were going to send his whole crew over seas. Ray's uncle in Port Arthur had a café and wanted Ray to take over operating it for him since he wanted to retire. Ray said that he did not want to go over seas, and that he was going to take the discharge from the service. He would be out of the army January 12th. About one more week, but he still had to get all their furniture and stuff out then. I told them I had just got off the phone to a ranch in central Texas and I had to be there Monday would be back Tuesday with a load of horses. We could help them all move. Well, 1949 had been a pretty good year, and I wondered what 1950 would be like...oh well, time will tell.

CHAPTER 12
1950

THURSDAY AND FRIDAY AND SATURDAY PAM and I would take the '49 panel truck and I had a '47 Ford pick up that Ray could drive. I could also take the sixteen-foot stock trailer and haul stuff in it. We could make a trip each day if we needed to. Ray looked surprised and said that would be a big help. They were looking at a house on El Paso Avenue not far from the café. They should be ready to go to Fort Polk by Thursday. Viola asked mother if she would keep Jere so she could go and help with the moving. Mother said sure and they could stay here until they got moved. Pam and I took everyone to our place and showed it to them since they hadn't seen it yet. Ray couldn't believe we made a living by training horses. I told them that was only part of it. We also made money rodeoing and other investments. Viola asked what kind of investments. I smiled and told them about Circle W Enterprises. We also raised corn with Uncle Jud for feed. We planted fifty to sixty acres of corn, about ten acres of purple hull peas, and about five acres of sweet potatoes every year. Then I told them about buying the Adams place next to Uncle Jud's It had about 250 acres with a house and a barn. Then I told them about the hundred and fifty acres of gravel land and selling gravel on it. Then we all went in our cabin and I got a box of mixed knives out and gave Ray and Viola and Jere each a knife. I told them about buying the knives. They liked the knives and thanked us for them and we sat around and visited for awhile. I told them about going to Fort Worth Rodeo the last part of January for seventeen days. Then we would go to the Houston Rodeo the last part of February that would also be for seventeen days. Monday morning Viola and Ray went looking at the house on El Paso.

We left for the Starr Ranch about 9:30 a.m. and took the sixteen-foot stock trailer. We stopped in Livingston at the saddle shop. The owners were glad to see us. He had taken in a rodeo bronc-riding saddle and wanted to get rid of it. I asked him how much he was asking for the bronc saddle and what would he sell all three for. He said $125.00 with used pads. I asked him how much to put adjustable stirrups on the two riding saddles. He said $7.50 each and he could have them ready in the morning. I told him we would pick all three up in the morning about 10.a.m. He said okay and he would have them ready. We got to the Starr Ranch about 2.p.m., Bill was glad to see us and we went out to look at the horses. Matt pointed at a roan and told me this horse had been dogged on at ranch rodeos. He was very fast and about 54 inches high. I told him I wanted this horse and three gentle riding horses, all sorrels. When I asked Bill how much per head he said $250.00 for the roan the roan and $150.00 each for the sorrels. I wrote him a check on the Circle W account. Then we put the horse in a pen and we all went to dinner and visited. I told him what all we had been doing. I went to the truck and got two boxes of mixed knives. I took them back in the diner. The women were all in the getting ready for the next guest to arrive. I told Bill to ask them all to come out. I put the knives on the table, out of their boxes   Bill's eyes opened wide and I told them to pick a knife, they were all free. I told Bill to pick one for his wife also because she was in office working. All the workers were family and they each picked a knife. About that time the horse wrangler came in for a break. He was not kin to anyone there but I called him over and gave him a knife also. Bill thanked us, and I told Bill to his pick his two nephews that supply meat for the guest ranch and for his brother and his wife. Bill asked why I was doing this. Then I told him about the knife deal and I was doing this because I wanted to. I had already given some away to my kinfolks and friends. They all thanked us for the knives.

A little while later we ate then we sat around and visited. Bill told us about a ranch close to Houston that has a stud horse that is Haflinger breed. These horses are from Austria and are light chestnut with a white mane and tail. They are all 52 to 56 inches tall. Haflinger is a well- built breed with deep girth, they are hard working, docile and intelligent. I looked at a picture of the horses and I liked them very much. Bill told me that he had four Welsh mares that he has taken to this stud. He hoped to improve his line of horses; he hoped he will get a good colt out of one of the four mares he has at the ranch. I asked him to let me know how the Welsh mares do and told him that I sure liked this Haflinger breed. Bill said he would let us know. The next morning we loaded up the three sorrels and one roan and for home. We stopped Livingston and got the saddles. He had put the adjustable stirrups on them. We got home about 2 p.m. I put the sorrels in one stall and gave them some feed and I put the roan in with Cody. They acted as if they knew each other. Wednesday we worked the sale and my sister and Ray had bought the house on El Paso Avenue. Thursday morning we hooked 16-foot rodeo trailer to the panel truck. It had a seat for two behind the driver and passenger seat. We took all our rodeo stuff out in case we needed the space. We got to Fort Polk about 9 a.m. and loaded all we could in the trailer and put some boxes of stuff in the panel truck. We got home and stopped by our place. Then we went to the house on El Paso and unloaded and went back to our place.

We decided we could haul the rest of their stuff with two trucks and a trailer. We cleaned out the 16-foot stock trailer we hauled horses in and hooked it to the '47 pickup since it had a five-speed transmission. Friday we left early and got to Fort Polk about 9.a.m. Ray went and got his discharge and we started loading. We got everything in the pickups and trailers. We got home and we were all tired, so we parked the trucks and trailers in the hall of the barn. Saturday we took everything to their house and put everything up. Monday we worked with Toby and Cody. Cody was doing real well. Pam worked Streak on the barrels. Toby worked well also. Wednesday we worked the sale and Herb and Dot and Joe, Cindy and Dub came to the sale. We decided everyone would come to our place in Nederland Monday and all leave together to go to Fort Worth. Sunday Homer and Norm drove up. They wanted to know if we were going to Fort Worth. I told him yes then told him about all of the people that were going. Homer and Norm wanted me to mount them in the dogging. Homer said that he would tell the gate man about all of us and he would have stickers for our windshields. We left out Monday morning and ate breakfast at the café by the sale barn in Beaumont. We got to Fort Worth and got all set up before dark. The rodeo started on Friday. We all made money and it ended on February 10th, a Sunday, and we all came home on Monday.

Tuesday morning about 8:30 a lady and her daughter, about fourteen years old drove up. They were looking for a gentle horse. Her daughter had a friend that was going to ride on the Salt Grass Trail ride to the Houston Livestock Show and Rodeo. I showed the lady the sorrel horses and told her they were very gentle and would work or ride. She saw the two-wheel cart with a roof and windshield. The lady was a little heavy to ride, but she liked the cart for herself. Pam saddled the 14-hand horse for the girl to ride. I hooked up the smaller horse to the two-wheel cart, got on the cart and the lady got on it with me. I showed her how to drive the cart. She said if she had this cart she could go on the rail ride, too. I told her that they had wagons on the trail ride and the cart would be ideal for the ride. After she drove the cart by herself, she asked how much for everything. I told her the saddle would be $450. The cart, horse and harness would be $650. She told me they had a trailer, but might think about a bigger trailer. I showed her the 16-foot stock trailer and told her it would haul the two horses and she could take the shafts off and put the cart up front. She thought a little bit about the 16-foot trailer and asked how much. Then she said she'd take the trailer also and asked how much I wanted for it. I told her $1000 for the trailer. I showed her how we slept in the trailers and used folding cots, and she liked that idea. She wrote me a check for all of it and we loaded everything in the trailer and they left.

Pam and I went to Nederland and put the check and some of the rodeo money in the bank. Eight days later we all met again and went to the Houston Livestock show and Rodeo. This time I entered the bareback riding, the saddle bronc riding, and the steer dogging. Pam entered the barrel racing. I was up in the bareback riding the first night. I drew a top horse named Lazy B. Everyone told me he was a good horse and I should place high in the bareback riding and they were right. I believe he was the stoutest horse I had ever ridden. There were 125 bareback riders and I scored 92 points and placed second in the first go around. If my second horse was a good bucker, I could win the average. We didn't get but two horses for the whole rodeo. I was not up until the last night. By then I had found out my last horse was not very good. I did not place at all on him, but I was happy just to win a second place at the Houston rodeo. I did make some money in the dogging, enough to make my entry fee back. I also made money mounting other doggers on my dogging team. Pam made money in the barrel racing. The last two go rounds there was a girl in barrel racing that had not made any money. Her horse was not fast enough. Pam found out her horse was twenty years old and had done his best. Pam asked her if she would like to use Streak for the last two go around. She said she sure would and that her horse just didn't have it anymore. She did place in the last two go rounds and she was so pleased about Streak that she asked Pam how much she would sell him for. Pam told her $4000 and she wrote Pam a check to the Circle W Enterprise account and loaded Streak in her trailer with her older horse.

We came home from Houston with Toby and Cody. I told Pam she could use the roan on barrels until we got another good barrel horse. Monday evening I called Big T Trailers and ordered two 16-foot trailers ($800.00 each) both with silver paint. Mr. T said that he would have one at the Kirbyville sale Wednesday and the other the next Wednesday. I told him that would be fine. Tuesday Harry and Arlene came out. He told us about the Texaco strike. He said it would be a bad strike and that the company was going to try and break the union. I told him that he could build wagons and carts and I would pay him for them. He thanked me and said he hoped the strike didn't last too long. I called Porter and asked him if he could use more help at the sale. He said sure and to bring Harry and Arlene, that she could help in the office. Wednesday we all went to the sale in the panel truck. A fellow was waiting for me. He had four acres next to the sale barn on the east side Highway frontage on the Bleakwood highway. The four acres was 2 acres wide and 2 acres deep. He said that he worked at Texaco and he needed the money because of the strike. I asked him how much an acre for the track. He said $1000 for the four acres. I ask him if he had the papers with him. He said he would see them in morning and we could go to the courthouse. I told him that the next morning would be fine. We spent the night in Pam's cabin at the sale barn. Thursday morning we all went to the courthouse and put the check for the four acres in the Circle W account. He had showed us the 6-inch pipe corner markers. Porter had a gate at the end of the lane that opens on to the four acres. He was glad that we had bought the four acres next to the sale barn. Uncle Jud wanted to know what we were going to do with the four acres. I told him I didn't know but when I figured it out I would let him know. The 16-foot stock trailer came in to the sale barn. I gave the driver a check for the trailers ($800 each). We waited until noon and after dinner we hooked up the new trailer and came home. Saturday morning Pam and I rode our mules to the fresh water canal and back. While we were riding I asked Pam what she thought about putting in a private butcher shop on the four acres. We weren't always happy about the meat we buy at the stores and we could buy steers at the sale and put them on corn and when they got the size we wanted we could butcher them. This way we would know we got our own beef. Pam liked the idea of the butcher shop. We talked about it all the way back home.

Monday Harry and Arlene came out. I told them about the butcher shop and building a fence on the four acres. Harry said sure. He thought it would give them something to do while the strike was on. I told him I would pay him the same as Texaco. Harry said that Arlene's job was slow because of the strike. Harry said that he walked the picket line on Mondays and Arlene goes to the office on Monday also. I told them they could take the 14-foot rodeo trailer and the '47 Ford pickup and stay on the 4 acres with it. Harry said they could build the fence on Tuesday through Friday and maybe Saturday. I asked them to go the pipe yard in Beaumont and see what they had. I figured if we put a pipe post every ten feet, we would need over 150 10-foot posts. Harry thought so too and he also thought we should put the post in concrete. We got to the pipe yard and asked about used pipe. I told the pipe man we were going to build a pipe fence. One pipe at the top would be 7-feet high and three sucker rods for bars. I told him we would need them to deliver the pipe to the sale barn at Kirbyville. He said he would deliver the pipe Tuesday after dinner.

Tuesday morning Harry and Arlene hooked the 14-foot rodeo trailer to the '47 pickup. I hooked the welding machine to the '49 panel truck and we all headed for Kirbyville. While we were waiting, Harry and I laid out the fence. I wanted a three-acre pasture on the back and I wanted about one acre on the front on the Bleakwood Highway. Porter saw us and walked over and I told him about putting in a butcher shop. I told Porter he could put a steer in the pasture also. I explained that we weren't always happy with the meat we get at the store. This way we should always have good meat and he liked this idea a lot. I asked Porter who I could get to drill a water well. He told me about a fellow that had drilled his well and I asked him to call the man. Porter said okay and he went to go call him right then. Harry and I went to a lumberyard and bought twenty sacks of concrete and had it delivered. We went back and picked a spot on the East Side close to where the butcher shop would be. When the man came to check on the drilling the well, I had it all picked out. When he got there, I asked him how deep he thought he would have to go. He told us that he always found good water about 100 feet. He would drill a six-inch well and put the pump down in the well and put the storage tank on a concrete slab. The well man said that he could drill the well Thursday and finish Friday with a 6X6 well house also. I told him that would be good. I told Harry to go ahead with the fence. I had to work the sale and he said okay.

Wednesday morning Pam and I were talking to Dub the horse-shoer. He was parked near the oak trees. We had started toward the sale barn. A fellow drove up with a 4X10 horse trailer. He stopped right by us. He asked if I would be interested in a good horse and trailer and some other things. "Well," I said, "let's see what you have." He unloaded a buckskin horse and saddle. He said the horse was part Missouri Fox Trotter and had a good fox trot. He had two spots on his neck, one on each side, about the size of a potato, so we named him Tater. I rode the horse and he did have a smooth gait (I always called it a single foot gait). Then he showed us a .410 shotgun, a leather saddle holster, and a pair of chaps. He used to coon hunt on the horse and he carried the .410 shotgun hunting and a Robeson two-blade trapper-folding knife with 440 stainless steel blades and stag handles. He also had a box of halters, ropes, and a pair of spurs. I asked him how much he wanted for everything. He said the horse, saddle, and trailer would be $300. The chaps were $10, the 410 shotgun and holster were $30, the box of tack was $10, and the two-blade trapper knife was $10, coming to a grand total of $360. I wrote him a check on the Circle W account. We unhooked the trailer from his truck and hooked it to the '49 panel truck. I did not tell anyone about the trapper knife. I wanted the knife myself. Pam said she wanted the .410 shotgun. I told her it was hers. The man also gave me a blue tick hound pup about two months old. I told Pam, she should ride Tater around and show him to Harry and Arlene. I would walk over and tell Uncle Jud. We both got back about the same time.

Pam went to the office and I unsaddled Tater and put the saddle in the storage part of the 4 x 10 trailer. Then I took Tater over to Dub and asked him to trim his hooves. When he got through I put him in the pen we used all the time. I told Uncle Jud about the blue tick pup. He said he would like to have the pup. I told him I did not need the pup he could sure have him. His name was Blue. I would put him in the 4 x 10 trailer and Uncle Jud could take him when he went home that evening. Also I would take Tater to the farm and have him to ride. Thursday I called the electric company and had electricity brought to a meter loop Friday evening we had the well finished and electricity to the well and could pump water. We all helped build the fence and went home Saturday morning. Uncle Jud took Blue to his farm and Blue took to Uncle Jud like a duck takes to water. He did not let Uncle Jud go anywhere without him. Uncle Jud got an old big towel and Blue bonded with that towel. Uncle Jud put the towel on the seat by him on the two-wheel cart. Blue rode on the seat when Uncle Jud drove the cart. Monday morning we went to Uncle Jud's to help crops. Blue rode along side Uncle Jud all morning. After dinner Uncle Jud asked me to hide in the barn. We wanted Blue to find me. I took one of my socks and handed it to Uncle Jud. I took the other sock and pinned it on my britches leg and I put on a clean pair of socks. Uncle Jud took Blue in the house and I went and hid in the barn. Uncle Jud took Blue to where my tracks were. He took my sock and laid it on my tracks. He then showed it to Blue and Uncle Jud kept showing and in a little while, Blue got what Uncle Jud wanted. Blue sniffed my tracks and followed my tracks to the barn. Uncle Jud petted Blue and gave him half a biscuit. Blue was happy. Then I petted him also. We kept this up of me going and hiding. Each time I would go further. Blue would track me each time and Uncle Jud always had a treat. Later Pam and I would go hide. Pam would go one direction and I would go another. Blue would not go far without Uncle Jud. Uncle Jud would go with Blue until the tracks divided. Blue would look at Uncle Jud. He would look at the tracks and point to the tracks he wanted Blue to follow. When Blue would find one of us, we would go back to the others' tracks and track them to find the other person. This training took several weeks.

The next week after I bought the buckskin saddle horse, a fellow came up to me on Wednesday morning at the sale barn. He was driving a 1946 John Deere tractor. He called it a Popping Johnny. It had a set of springs with hand lift disk on the tractor. He asked me if I would be interested in buying the tractor. I told him maybe and that it depended on how much he was asking. He told me he wanted $450. I told him I couldn't pay that. I offered $400 for the tractor and disk and he said okay. Harry and Arlene were building the fence on the four acres. I drove the tractor around there and showed them. Harry liked the tractor a lot. He looked at the disk and told he thought he could make a clamp on hitch on the tractor and could pull a trailer. I told him it would be good if we could pull trailers with it here at the sale barn. Uncle Jud liked the tractor too. I told him he could haul manure to the four acres with the tractor.

We worked the sale and built the fence on the four acres. Friday evening we all went home to Nederland. Saturday Brownie drove up with a trailer. I asked Brownie what he had in the trailer. He told me he had a nice sorrel mare that was three-years old. He had bought one ticket on a raffle and won the mare but he wanted to sell her. She was a registered Haflinger. I asked him how much. He said he would take two hundred for the mare and he had the papers with him. I wrote him a check on the Circle W account. I also gave Brownie one of the Queen knives like I had given the others. He saw the knife and smiled and thanked me. We visited a while and then he left. I put the mare in a stall and gave her some feed. Monday and Tuesday we went to Uncle Jud's and planted corn and peas. We worked the sale Wednesday. Thursday we all built fence on the four acres. I called Bill about the Haflinger mare. He wanted to know if I would sell the mare. I told him no, but that I would trade the mare for geldings. Bill said that was even better. Then he asked how many geldings I wanted for the mare and I told him I would leave that up to him. I would like to bring the mare Monday if it would be okay and he said Monday would be good. So, Monday we loaded the mare in a 16-foot stock trailer and we got to the Starr ranch about 3 p.m. Bill looked at the mare and said he liked the mare real well and would trade four geldings for the mare. Matt showed me a gray roan gelding about fifteen hands tall. The horse was the same color as Toby and Cody. I told Pam that this horse would make a good barrel horse. She thought so, too. Then Matt showed me a dapple-gray that was a little over fourteen hands high. He had black legs and a black head. This horse really stood out. I told Matt I would take him. The next two could be gentle sorrels that would work and ride. This would be four head and would be a load. We named the gray roan Sandy and we named the dapple-gray Chip. The two sorrels we did not name. We visited the rest of the evening. The next morning we loaded the four geldings and headed home. We stopped in Livingston at the saddle shop and bought two saddles. We got home about 2 p.m. Wednesday we worked the sale. Thursday we planted corn. Friday we helped build fence on the four acres. Saturday we started training Sandy on barrels. I rode Chip and taught him to rein some.

E.C. came by because he needed to move his cows to another pasture. I asked him when he wanted to move them and how much help he needed. E.C. said he had over 300 head and would need lots of help. Also his brother and his son wanted to help. He had sold his horse and he needed two gentle horses if I had them. I told E.C. I had two sorrel horses and saddles and he could use them. I would get some good help, Herb and Dot and Joe and Cindy. E.C. told us to meet him at the pasture next Saturday about sun up. I told him to tell V.C. and his son to come here Friday evening. I would have the two sorrel horses here. E.C. thanked me a lot and said he would tell his brother, and that they could sleep here in their trailer. There would be probably three others camping here and we would take our horses in trailers to the pasture on the Beaumont Highway. After E.C. left I called the LeBlanc brothers in Port Arthur and told them about the cattle drive and to bring L.A. also. They could meet here Friday and camp here and we would trailer our horses about seven miles to the cow pasture and drive them about seven miles. I also called Clyde and told him about the cattle drive and asked him to bring Tony and his son. Clyde said that they would meet us at the pasture on Saturday. Monday we went to Uncle Jud's and helped plant corn and peas. Tuesday we helped build fence on the four acres and we got a bid on the butcher shop and told the man to go ahead and get started. Wednesday we worked the sale barn. Thursday and Friday morning we helped build fence on the four acres and came home after dinner.

Friday evening we got ready for the cattle drive. Herb and Dot and Joe and Cindy came out. Herb did not have a horse so I told him about Chip and said he could use him to ride. Pam and I would ride our mules. The LeBlanc brothers and L.A. came out and camped also. V.C. and his son camped with us. Harry rode Bill and Arlene rode Pedro on the cattle drive. I showed V.C. the sorrels they could ride. V.C. asked if they could ride a little here and get used to the two horses. I told them sure and we saddled them up and rode around some. Herb saddled Chip and he really liked him. Saturday morning we loaded up and trailered our stock to the pasture to start the drive. Tom Smith was there with his daughter and grandson who were going to help on the drive. Tom had his stock trailer and follower along. He would put baby calves that got tired in the stock trailer. We drove the cows out on to Highway 365 and drove them about four miles west. We crossed the fresh water canal and a railroad track, and then turned right on the old Port Acres to Beaumont Highway. We drove the cows about four miles to a big pasture on the left. Pam and I and E.C. were up front. I was riding Gray Boy. Cows will follow a gray horse well. E.C. had the gate open and I rode in and cows followed. Tom had about ten calves that had gotten tired in the trailer. He got the calves out and the cows started looking for their babies.

E.C. rode up to Pam and me and told us he wanted to do something for all the help. He asked about having a bar-b-que on Sunday at our place. We said sure, we thought everyone would like it. I asked E.C. how about the next day at about 3 or 4 p.m. We needed time to cook the meat. Harry had built a good size bar-b-que grill on a two-wheel trailer. E.C. thought 3 or 4 would be a fine time. He gave us a hundred dollars and said if it wasn't enough we should let him know. He then told everyone to come eat at our place tomorrow about 4 p.m. and to bring their family. We all rode back to our trailers. On the way V.C. and his son rode up to us and thanked us for the horses they rode. Then he asked if the horses and saddles were for sale and if so, how much. I told him that yes I would sell them and that each horse and saddle would be $450. He said okay, he would take them home this evening and they would see us tomorrow. Harry and Arlene and Pam and I all went to the store and got an assortment of meat to cook, and lots of hamburger buns. Sunday evening we had all that helped plus wives and kids. We had a bunch to show up. My folks came over and ate with us as well.

Monday, Harry worked the strike picket line and Arlene worked at her job. Pam and I went to Uncle Jud's to plant corn and peas. Tuesday we finished planting then Pam and I worked the sale Wednesday and helped to build more fence. Friday evening we all came home. Later, Harry called me because Arlene's uncle who lived in Alvin, Texas had a ranch and needed Harry and Arlene to help and stay about a week. Harry wanted to know if they could take Pedro and Bill to use working cows. I told Harry sure and they could take the 14-foot rodeo trailer and the '47 pickup with a four-speed transmission. Harry said okay and they would see us in the morning. Saturday morning Harry and Arlene came out and loaded up and headed for Alvin.

We rode Gray Boy and Star to the sale barn in Beaumont. Monday we trained Sandy on barrels and I rode Chip, the new gray horse. Tuesday evening we went to Kirbyville. I drove the Popping Johnny tractor and disked the three acres. Wednesday we worked the sale. Thursday we planted Bermuda grass on the three acres, and Friday we hauled manure to the Adams Place. Saturday, Harry and Arlene came back from Alvin, Texas. I started calling all the riders that had been going on the Spring Trail Ride and telling them the ride would be on Saturday the 18th. Some would meet here and all travel together. We all had a good time. Each year we have about ten more riders. Ed Brown put out a five-gallon bucket for donations. We were going to use them towards expenses. Sunday morning we all went home. Wednesday we went to the sale and after the sale we worked on cross fence. We had a shed on each side of the cross fence all together. This way the steers could get out of the weather and have a place to eat. We had the entire pipe fence painted. Friday we all went home. I called the same fence man that put the chain link fence on our pens in Nederland. I had already shown him the four acres. He said he would start on the fence next week. Friday evening, Homer and Norm and "T" with the Diamond S rodeo company drove up and told us they had two rodeos going on at the same time, one in Waco and one in Gladewater. Homer and Norm would be the pickup men at Waco. "T" would need two pickup men at Gladewater. Homer asked if I would be a pickup man and asked if I could get another pickup man. I told them I could be one pickup man and Harry could be the other. "T" asked if we had pickup horses. I told him yes, that I would show him the horses. We walked over to the pens back of the cabin and we showed him Buckskin Bill and Chip, the new dark gray horse. I asked "T" when this rodeo was. He told me the rodeo would start Tuesday night and will be each night with two shows Saturday and we'd come home Sunday.

I called the fence man and had him go ahead and put 6-foot chain link fence on the four acres. I told him that we would be out of town and would call him when we got back. He said okay and that he would just do like he did on our place. I called Herb and told him about Gladewater. He said they would go and would call Joe and Cindy. Sunday we all met here and headed to Gladewater and got all set up. I locked four stalls for our horses. I asked Herb if he would like to ride Chip for the Grand Entry. He said yes, that they had only brought Dot's barrel horse and he would take care of Chip like he was his own. Herb and I entered the saddle bronc riding and dogging. When I was up in the bronc riding Herb would be the pickup man. We all made good money and headed home Sunday. When we got home the Texaco strike and ended. Monday morning Harry went back to work.

When the Big Boss from Houston saw all the mules he told them to sell them. They would replace them with tractors. A fellow named Joe Green took care of the mules seven days a week. He had a room in the barn next to the tack room. There were seventeen head of mules. One mule was a red sorrel and with a white mane and tail. He was about a year and half old. There were 8 blacks 15 hands high, 4 red mules, 4 gray mules, and 1 sorrel 1-½ years old. Joe and the young mule got along real well. He was in a group that was bought at the Fort Worth mule sale. A fellow named Wally that worked for Texaco bought all the mules and tack and equipment. He picked the two 15-hand black mules and wanted to sell the rest. Harry worked at the mule barn as maintenance foreman that worked with the mules. When Wally said he wanted to sell the rest, Harry gave me a call. Pam and I drove out to the Texaco mule barn and looked at the mules. Harry told me that Joe Green had become attached to the young sorrel mule and he sure wanted him. I told Harry if I could make a deal on everything I would give the young mule to Joe. Joe was the caretaker of the mules; he kept their hooves trimmed and fed them. He also kept the movers oiled and greased. Wally came up and told me all equipment went with the mules; this included twenty collars and reins, ten saddles of different sizes, ten mule drawn sickle mowers, and lots of hand tools, anvils, and clippers. Harry and I and Wally all walked over to the mules. Wally had already taken his pair of 15-hand mules and a wagon home. All the mules were about 14-hand high. There were 6 black mules, 4 gray mules, 4 red mules, and the mule that Joe Green wanted that was red and about 2 years old. I bought all of the mules for seventeen hundred dollars, as I figured that was what Wally had paid for all the mules. Wally would get his pair of mules free. This was still a good buy for me so I bought all fifteen head and gave the young red mule to Joe Green.

I told Joe I would give him the mule to help get the other mules and equipment to our place in Nederland. He could also take his pick of the saddles. Joe was happy about getting a saddle to go with his mule. He told me that he was going to retire from Texaco. He had been here twenty-five years and Texaco offered a good retirement package. I looked at Joe and he looked like he could be Native American. So I asked him and he said yes, he was full-blooded Cherokee. I did not tell him Pam was part Choctaw. Joe told me his full name was Joe Green Feather and that he had dropped "Feather" to work at Texaco. I wrote Wally a check on the Circle W account. Joe told me he was to stay until the mules left. I told Joe he and his mule could stay at our place. I might know of a job working with mules and horses. Joe said that would be good. He would like to work with mules and horses. Harry told us all the mules would work and ride and that he and Arlene could help get the mules to our place. I told him good, we would start hauling some things tomorrow. We would leave the mules and saddles until the last. We would ride and lead the mules Saturday. Pam and I went home and got a 16-foot stock trailer. We hauled a little bit of everything .We left the mules and saddles until Saturday. Tuesday we went to the Kirbyville sale and I told Uncle Jud about buying the mules and equipment. Then he asked me if I would buy his farm. I told him sure and he could stay on the place as long as he wanted. We could go the courthouse Thursday and transfer the deed to the circle W Enterprises. We worked the sale and spent the night with Uncle Jud .Thursday we had the paper work done on Uncle Jud's place. I wrote him a check for his equity then went the bank and paid off the note on the place.

Friday we hauled more equipment from the Texaco barn. Joe helped load and unload. I showed Joe the tack room and it would be his room and he could help take care of the mules here just like at the Texaco mule barn. Joe took his knife and cut notch on each mule's mane that worked and stayed together, about six inches from the shoulder. Next pair the notches was about eight inches from the shoulder and so on all the mules. We hauled things all day Friday. Dad looked at Joe and said something in Indian language. Joe looked at dad and smiled. I had never heard Dad say anything in Cherokee language before. Joe answered back in Cherokee. I looked at Dad and I knew he was part Cherokee. I asked him if he could speak fluid Cherokee. He said no just some words. Joe said he could speak fluid Cherokee. I said that was good, I would like to learn some Cherokee. I went and got a cot with springs and help Joe set up a place to sleep in the tack room. Saturday Harry and Arlene came out to help with the mules. Dad went with us, so he could drive the truck back. Harry and Arlene each rode a gray pair and I each rode a red pair. Joe rode a black mule and led a black mule like we did. I put this bunch of mules in back of our cabin. Dad took us all back after dinner. We had four black mules left. Joe rode his two year old mule. We all rode the last four mules. Joe's mule did well. I had a lead rope snap to the red mules halter. The red mule settled down and we all rode home. I called the Walker Brothers about the six black mules. They were very interested and said they would be there in about two hours. In a while they drove up with a long gooseneck type trailer. They looked at the mules and asked how much a head for all six head. I told them if they would take all six head I would sell them for $300.00 each. They said ok. They had called Colorado and they wanted all of them and we would leave Monday morning with all six head. They would not wait until September. I told them good and they wrote me a check for the mules.

We still had the sickle mowers to haul but I decided to get them later. I called Ed Brown and told him about the mules He asked how much and I told him all were the same price, $300.00 each. Ed told me the Guest ranch needed four more head and could we bring them Monday morning with the saddles. I told Ed we would bring the mules to the guest ranch if he wanted. He said he would meet us there and he needed saddles too. Then I told him about Joe Green. Ed said bring him he could sure use some more help. I told Joe to get his stuff together. I had him a job at the guest ranch. I told him about the Caddo Indians that lived on the river and that Ed Brown had helped the Caddos a lot. Also that some Cherokee's and Choctaws were living with Caddo's. Joe said he didn't know there were any Cherokee or Choctaw around here. Monday morning we loaded up the red mules and saddles for them. We got to the Guest ranch about 9.A.M. Layne Hill and his nephew were glad to see the mules. They were short of horses and had to let guests ride there personal ones. Layne said he and his nephew would ride mules. I told them we had four gray mules about the same size that would work and ride and asked if they needed some more. Layne said the guests liked horses better than mules. Layne said he was beginning to like mules better also.

While Layne was showing Joe around and where to put his mule and saddle, Ed asked me how much and wrote me a check on the Guest ranch account, then Pam and I went to Nederland. While we were at the Gladewater rodeo, Uncle Jud had taken the John Deere tractor and disks to the four acre feed lot and planted common Bermuda grass. The grass was now up and growing well. Tuesday we went to the Kirbyville sale. We walked over to look at the four acres of Bermuda grass. Porter and rest of us were looking at some calves to be sold. We liked two steer calves that were about 300 pounds. We decided we would each buy one and put them on the Bermuda grass. They should be ready to butcher by November. After the sale we wormed the calves and put them on the three acre side. After the sale we went home to haul more equipment from the Texaco mule barn. Saturday we got through with hauling the rest of equipment.

Monday we went to Uncle Jud's and hauled corn and peas. We also trained Blue, the pup I had given Uncle Jud. We decided we would ride the two gray gaited donkeys to the Kirbyville sale. As we rode by Ed Brown's office we saw his orange flag was out so we stopped to see him. Ed told Pam and me he had talked to the school board and they were going to sell some school buses. He wanted us to ride with him and Mrs. Brown to the Caddo village on the Sabine River. He wanted to ask the chief if they would like the buses to live in. We would haul our donkeys and mules as close as we could. Ed had not put a bridge across the creek yet, that the logging crew should get it in soon. We asked Ed when he wanted to ride to the Caddo. Ed asked if we could go Saturday and we told him Saturday would be fine. We had a trailer at Uncle Jud's and would ride these two donkeys here Saturday and all leave from here. We then rode on to the sale barn. After the sale we rode back to Uncle Jud's and hauled corn Thursday and Friday. Saturday we rode to the Caddo village on the river. The chief was glad to see us. Ed asked the chief about the buses to live in. They could take out the seats and put in a wood burning heater and also put some bunk beds in. The chief liked the idea. He said the winter is pretty cold. Ed said as soon as the loggers can put the bridge across the creek, he would bring the buses in and the chief was pleased. We rode back across the creek and on to our trailers. We went back to Uncle Jud's and told him what Ed Brown was going to do. Uncle Jud said the Caddo needed all the help they could get. We then went home to Nederland. We went to rodeos nearly every weekend all summer, along with Harry and Arlene. Our dogging team was doing well and Sandy, Pam's barrel horse, was doing good, also. Harry was a pickup man and Arlene rode Pedro the donkey in barrel racing. The butcher calves were doing well. They could not keep the Bermuda grass down. Porter and I decided we should put two more calves with the others. There were some nice calves at the sale so we picked put a couple and put them on the three acres. Ed got the bridge across the creek and put four school buses in the Caddo village for them to live in.

The first part of August, Bill Starr called on a Sunday right after dinner. He told me about a cougar that had killed some goats next door. A government lion hunter was going to be there Monday morning with his lion dogs and would try to catch the lion alive and move him to the Davis Mountains in west Texas. Bill wanted Pam and me to load up and be there Sunday evening so we could all go on the cougar hunt. He also said he had two black mules ready and we could ride them on the hunt. I told Bill Starr we would leave in about one hour. We got the Starr ranch before dark, and Bill and Matt showed us the two black mules. They were about 14-hands high. I liked the mules and asked Bill how much for them. He said $300 each. I said okay then asked him to show us a couple of horses to use in rodeos. Matt showed us a good-looking roan horse about 14-hands high. Matt said he was very fast and he came from the ranch a couple of miles from there. The same place they had gotten good horses from in the past. Then Matt showed us a roan horse about 15-hands high that came from the same ranch. I asked how much for them and Bill said $300 each. We put the roans in a pen together. I wrote Bill a check for $1200 for the four heads. About 8 p.m. a truck drove up. It was the lion hunter and we all introduced ourselves. Then we all set around and talked. Jim, the lion hunter, asked if we had any pellet guns. I told him I had a .177 caliber hand pump Crossman pistol. He said that he had some .177 caliber darts that would put the cat to sleep for about one hour. Try to shoot the cat in the hip if possible. I told him I had shot the pellet gun a lot and it was very accurate. I went and got the pellet pistol as well as a holster for it I had made out of four-inch belting. Jim got two of his .177 caliber darts and we put one dart in the pistol. The other he put in a safe container.

We sat around and talked until bedtime. Pam and I slept in our 16-foot stock trailer like we did at rodeos. The next morning we were up and riding at daylight. Pam and I rode the black mules. Jim rode his red mule. Jim had a friend with him who drove a truck and pulled a trailer with the dogs and another mule if he needed him. Bill Starr rode in the truck and Matt rode a gray mule. Bill showed us where the goat had been killed. Jim turned the hounds loose and they picked up the trail. The hounds continued trailing along the river. Jim decided he would cross the river and try to get ahead of the cat and he asked us to spread out. Matt stayed by the river, while, Pam and I headed east. We went about a mile and turned south and then we stopped and listened. We figured the hounds were going south. The cat was making a big loop. The hounds chased the cat until after dinner. We all had biscuits and ham with us so we could eat when we wanted.

Pam and I stopped and listened while we each ate a biscuit and ham. In a while we could hear the hounds headed our way. Pam and I spread out about three hundred yards apart. The hounds treed about a mile from us, so I started for the hounds. I looked in Pam's direction and saw her headed towards me. We rode up as quiet as possible. The cat was up a big cedar tree about fifteen feet away. Pam rode up and stopped while I rode around on the other side, and I eased up real slow. I could see the truck and Jim headed our way. I had already pumped my air pistol five times. I had a good shot at the hip of the cat so I aimed real good and hit him where Jim said to shoot him. Jim rode up and dropped a lead rope with some kind of anchor on it. He caught his dogs one by one and tied them. By this time the cat had gone to sleep and had lodged itself between two limbs. Jim got a rope and climbed the tree. He put his rope around the body so it would not choke the cat. Then he eased the cat down through the limbs. I got off my mule and let Pam hold him while Jim let the end of the rope go to me. We got the cat down and over to an eight-foot cage and Jim put a tag in the lion's ear. Jim and his partner checked the lion and wrote down his measurements then checked its teeth. We all got around the lion and pulled and pushed him into the cage. The lion was still out but started to wake up just as we finished.

By the time we got back to the Starr ranch it was almost dark. We all ate and talked about the hunt. I gave Jim the extra dart I had and he wanted to know more about me and Pam and us riding mules. I told him about some of my mules and training them. Then he told us, "When I first saw y'all I figured you would just be in the way and not be any help, but I was sure wrong. I have never had help that was as good as both of you have been. I thanked him and told him this was our first mountain lion hunt. When we help someone we try to be good help and we really enjoyed the hunt. He then told us he would be glad to have us anytime. Matt and Bill said they knew we would be good help and told Jim about us buying horses and mules from them and that we both competed in rodeos. I told Jim if he ever went to Fort Worth or the Houston Livestock Show and Rodeo, to look us up. We would try to get him tickets to see the rodeo. Jim said that when Bill said we competed in rodeos he figured small stuff, "But I was wrong. If ya'll ride at those shows that's big time." I told him Pam works, and she barrel races and hazes for me in the dogging and I also rode saddle broncs. I was not as good as the top twenty cowboys, but I get lucky every once in a while. We talked on and went to bed about 9 p.m.

We all got up early. I think that lion roared all night. We said our good-byes and we loaded up and headed for Nederland. We got home about noon and unloaded the two black mules and the two rodeo horses. I called the Walker brothers and told them we had two black mules for them. They said they would pick them up Thursday morning. I said that would be good. Wednesday we went to the sale at Kirbyville. We told Uncle Jud and Porter about the cat hunt and the mules we brought back. Thursday morning Pam and I started working the roan horses. All the horses that we bought from central Texas were good horses. They learned quickly and were very smart. The Walkers drove up about 9 a.m. I told them about riding the mules on the cat hunt and how well the mules rode. They asked how much on the mules. I told them $450 each. They wrote me a check to the Circle W account. They said they would take them to Colorado in September.

We worked the roan horses teaching them to rein and turn. I called Tom Smith and asked him if he had any young steers that needed training to run. He said yes, he had ten head we could practice on. How about bringing them Saturday morning? I told him Saturday would be good. I called Herb and Dot and asked them if they wanted to be here. They said yes and they would tell Joe and Cindy. We all got set up and Tom brought the steers. I wanted to try the roan horses on steers. Pam would haze on Chip. We also worked Toby and Cody. Dot would haze for Herb and Cindy would haze for Joe. Tom loaded up his steers and took them home. He had the steers sold to a rodeo contractor when they got older. Joe told me he was always having trouble with his1948 panel truck and asked if I would sell him my 1949 panel truck because he knew someone who wanted his '48. I told him yes that I had been thinking about hauling four horses and getting a ¾ ton truck. Joe knew my 1949 panel truck was a good truck so he bought the 1949 and drove it home I told Pam we would use the '47 pickup until we could get a '51 ¾ ton. Tuesday morning Pam and I drove to Kirbyville to talk to the Ford dealer. We asked him when the 1951 trucks would be available. He told us about the first part of September and asked what kind we were wanting. He said he could put in the order. I told him we wanted a ¾ ton truck with a 12-foot flat bed and a five-speed transmission, floor shift. He suggested the F3-3/4ton, six-cylinder motor. He could get a factory 12-foot steel bed and a heavy duty bumper. It would pull a trailer well. I told him ok and to get a price on the truck. He said he would let us know.

We then drove over to the sale barn. Porter was there and walked over to us. Then Herb and Dot and Joe and Cindy all drove up. Dub was there, too. Porter told us of a rodeo, that the rodeo contractor in Sulphur, Louisiana had called him. The rodeo would be that Friday night and Saturday afternoon and Saturday night. He would need a lot of cowboys. He wanted to know if we could all go. The rodeo was in McComb, Mississippi. He and his family were going and would leave Thursday morning. It would probably take about 7-8 hours to get there. A.J., the rodeo contractor, was almost begging. Porter said A.J.

would need dogging teams and roping and barrel racers. I told him that Pam and I would go. Herb said they would all go. I asked them to all meet at our place and leave Thursday morning. Herb said that would be good. We all worked the sale and went home Wednesday evening. We all decided to camp at our place Wednesday night and leave together. Dub said he would go. Herb and them went home and got their horses then came to our place. We were all talking about taking extra horses. I asked Herb if they wanted to pull one of my 16-foot stock trailers. Pam and I were going to take Toby and Cody and Sandy. Dub had gone by the café near the Beaumont sale barn. Just as Dub sat down at a table, Norm walked in. Dub waved him over. Norm told him the Diamond S didn't have a rodeo that weekend, so he came in. He had his rodeo gear at the tack room at the sale barn. Dub told him about the rodeo in McComb and asked if he wanted to go. Dub was headed to our place because we were all leaving in the morning. Norm said sure, he would go get his stuff and be right back. Dub and Norm drove up and we were glad to see them both. I told Dub that he could pull the 4x10 trailer and I had a folding cot to put in the trailer and Norm would have a place to sleep.

Herb and Dot only had one horse, a barrel horse. I had the roan horses. They were a dogging team there. Then Joe said he could take another horse because they just had two. I told them I had a good all around gray horse (Chip) that we might need. This way we all had three horses to take. We went and unhooked Herb's 12-foot trailer and hooked up the silver 16-foot stock trailer. We pulled our 16-foot rodeo trailer. Joe pulled his 16-foot stock trailer. We all loaded up and left about 4 a.m. Thursday. We got to McComb, Mississippi about noon Thursday. Porter and his family drove up shortly after. We all set up together. A.J. was there and was glad we were all there too. He told us there was not enough cowboys around and asked us to work all events that we could. I had never roped calves at a rodeo, just when working cows. I entered calf-roping, bareback, saddle bronc, and dogging. I didn't make any money in the calf roping. The fastest time I had was sixteen flat and that wasn't near fast enough. It was good to fill in and put on a show. We all helped each other in all the events and we all made good money. It was one show on Friday night and one Saturday evening and one Saturday night. Sunday morning as we were all getting ready to leave the rodeo, the rodeo committee walked up. They wanted to thank us for working all the events. If we had not, the rodeo would not have been a success. We said we were all glad to help. A.J. came up then and thanked us all for being there. Then we all headed home.

The Alexandria rodeo was next, the last part of August. We took the roan horses for a dogging team and Pam took the sorrel horse. These horses needed more training. We planned to take them to the Texarkana Four-State Fair and Rodeo. We went to the Alexandria rodeo and made good money with the roan horses. They were making a good tea. We came home from Alexandria Sunday morning. Tuesday we went to the Kirbyville dealership to order a new truck. The dealer said we should get a ¾ ton with a 12-foot flat bed. The dealer said that the 1951 ¾ ton would be there the last part of September. I told him good because we would need it to go to Dallas for all of October. We went to the sale barn and worked the sale. We all decided we would meet the next Monday, spend the night there, and leave early Tuesday for Texarkana. We were going to take the roans and the sorrel horse. We got to Texarkana Tuesday after dinner. We picked out place to set up. I went and locked three stalls for our horses. Wednesday morning cowboys started arriving. I knew there would be a lot at the rodeo. Pam and I were brushing our horses and talking. In a few minutes I heard a mule bray. I looked at Pam and said, "I haven't heard a mule bray at a rodeo in a long time." The mule bray sounded like it was about 100 yards from us. We decided to saddle up and ride over and see for sure. As we rode up I saw a gray mule tied to a trailer. I got off my roan horse and walked over and introduced myself. The man that had the mule was a man named Harley. I looked at the mule's right hind leg and I knew it was Jake. Jake was trying to get to me. I walked over and petted him on his neck and called his name. Harley said, "That mule acts like he knows you."

I told Harley he should know me since I used to own him. His name was Jake when I owned him. Harley said his name was still Jake. When he bought Jake, he was real fast, and he made good money with him. Now he acted like he was not interested in dogging at all. I told him Jake didn't look too good and I thought something was wrong with him. He told me the fellow that had been hazing for him would not be there; he would need a hazer. I told him I would haze for him. I showed him the sorrel horse that Pam was riding. The sorrel had been hazed on and was really fast. Harley and I became good friends. He had a wife at home in Oklahoma and she was planning on going to Dallas for all of October. He asked if we were going to Dallas and I told him yes and that we had been before. I asked Harley if he would like to move his trailer over next to us before it got too crowded. Harley said yes, that it was nice of us to invite him to do so. We worked together all through the rodeo. Harley had only placed on one steer; it was a set up steer. The steer would run about 40-50 feet and stop. Jake ran right by and Harley was ready and leaned over and dropped the steer in five seconds flat and won a second place. Jake just wasn't trying. I told Harley that if he wanted, he could use the roan horse on his last three steers. Harley said okay because he needed to make some money and it seemed like he wasn't going to on Jake. Everyone that had used the roan was making money. Harley placed on all three heads on the roan.

The last day of the rodeo, Harley asked if I would sell him the roan horse and if I'd take Jake in on trade. I told Harley I would sell him the roan. The price was $2500. I would take Jake and allow him $500 and he would owe me $2000, but he wouldn't owe me anything for using the roan on his last three heads. Harley thought that was a fair price on the roan. He also wanted to know if we would be taking the roan that I hazed on to Dallas. I told him I could bring him and we had another dogging team at home. Harley said that his wife was planning to go too. Pam told him his wife could use the roan, he ran barrels, too. We had another barrel horse at home as well (Chip). Harley wrote me a check for the roan. I walked over and brought Jake back and tied him to the trailer. I put Jake up front in the trailer and the roan hazing horse next, Jake almost ran to get in the trailer. I told everyone we would stop in Kirbyville and check on our ¾ ton truck. We got there about six hours later. Dub stopped also. He said it was no use to go to Beaumont and drive back Tuesday. He would stay here and go home Thursday. Dub parked at his usual place by the oak trees. We unloaded Jake and the two horses. Then we unhooked the trailer. We needed to go to the bank and to the Ford dealer, our ¾ ton was supposed to be there. I deposited the check for the roan horse and some more. When we drove up to the Ford dealership, our ¾ ton was sitting out front. It was dark green and had a 12-foot steel bed on it with a heavy-duty trailer hitch. The dealer was glad to see us. I paid him $3000 for the truck.

Pam drove the '47 pickup and I drove the '51 ¾ ton truck back to the sale barn. I had asked Dub to trim Jake's hooves while we were gone. He had Jake all ready when we got back. I hooked the rodeo trailer to the new truck. I loaded Jake last and drove to Uncle Jud's. Uncle Jud came out and looked at the ¾ ton truck. He sure liked it. Then I unloaded Jake and Uncle Jud was really surprised to see him. He did not think he would ever see Jake again. Uncle Jud looked at Jake and said he didn't look good and I agreed. Uncle Jud said he might have worms. He looked in his mouth and saw that Jake's gums were pink. Uncle Jud told me to go to Newton and buy two tubes of worm paste. He wanted to treat Jake for worms. He said he would worm him at four different times. If he wormed all at once it might kill all the worms too quick and he couldn't pass them and it would kill Jake. He said by killing a few at a time, Jake would be okay. The second tube we bought for later on. He then looked at Jake's teeth again and saw a wolf tooth at the back of Jake's teeth. Uncle Jud said that is part of his trouble. A wolf tooth would drive some horses crazy.

Uncle Jud and I were talking about butchering the calves. They had just been on the feed lot about 100 days. He wanted to butcher ours Wednesday after the sale. We would dress him out and hang him up in the cooler until Saturday morning. Then process him, which would probably take all morning. I told him that would be fine. I wanted him to take a lot of meat. I told Porter about the calves and asked if he wanted to do his calf as well. He said his boys wanted to help and as soon as they came home from school Wednesday, they would be over. I told Uncle Jud and Porter we would go home and be back Wednesday morning and work the sale. We would butcher the calves after the sale. We got home and I brought my folks up to date about Jake and butchering the calves. I told them we would bring them some meat Saturday. Wednesday morning we left early and drove the ¾ ton to Kirbyville. Uncle Jud and Porter were there already. We drove the steers through the sale ring so we could weigh them. When we bought them one steer weighed 240 and the other 235. This time they weighed 540 and 535. They had each gained three pounds a day. After the sale we butchered the steer that I had bought. He dressed out about 325 pounds. We quartered him up and hung him up in the cooler. Just then, Porter and his boys drove up. We helped them a little, and put their steer in the cooler also. We went home that evening. Thursday we rode Toby, the dogging horse, and Cody, the hazing horse in the morning. We rode the roan barrel horse and Chip in the evening. They needed to be in good shape for the Dallas rodeo, Friday we rode them again. Harry and Arlene came out Friday evening. We brought them up to date on everything. We told them we were going to the butcher shop in the morning so we could process the meat. They said they wanted to go, too. I had already told them they could have some of the meat. We got an ice chest from my folks, plus we had two ice chests and Harry and Arlene had one in their cabin. Pam and I had talked about buying a chest type deep freeze. We decided to stop in Kirbyville and buy one. Harry and Arlene spent the night in their cabin.

We all got up early and got to Kirbyville about 7:30 in the morning. We all had on older work clothes to process the beef. We all went to an appliance store in Kirbyville to look at a deep freeze. The salesman had a nice freeze a ten cubic foot one. I asked him how much and he told me $250. I told him okay I would take it. He looked at us in our work clothes. He said he would have to have credit information before we would sell me the deep freeze. I told the storeowner he did not need my credit information. He said yes he did and he could not sell us the freezer without it. I told him okay and turned around and we all went to the truck. I turned and told the man to call the Ford dealership and tell him we came by in a '47 maroon pickup and you wouldn't sell us a freezer.

We left and went to another appliance store in Kirbyville. They had a deep freeze all hooked up and it was real quiet. He was real nice and the price was the same. I wrote him a check on the Circle W account from the Kirbyville bank. We backed up and loaded the deep freeze on the '47 pickup. We drove to the butcher shop and backed up to the front door. Harry and I pushed the freezer inside and plugged it in. Uncle Jud and Aunt Willie were already there. We processed the two hindquarters first. We wrapped the steaks and some roast first and put them in the freezer. We put the eye of the round roast in the freezer also. We ground up the rest into hamburger meat. Porter and his boys drove up and started on their beef. Mrs. Porter and her mother and dad drove up later. Uncle Jud showed them how to cut up the beef. They wanted their beef cut up like we did. I told Uncle Jud to take about a third of the meat to his house because Pam and I ate a lot at his place. If he ran out of meat I would bring some from our house. We cut up all but one shoulder and left it in the walk-in cooler. Uncle Jud said he would cut it up later. Porter left one shoulder also. We went home Saturday evening and came back Monday and got some more of the meat. We gave Harry and Arlene some of the beef also.

Monday evening we got ready to go to the Dallas State Fair and Rodeo. We took Toby and Cody for a dogging team and Pam took Chip for barrel racing. We took the roan horse also. I figured Harley's wife would want him to haze on and run barrels. We used the new ¾ ton truck to pull the trailer with four horses. The new truck did real well. Dub used the 4 x 10 trailer to sleep in at Dallas. We got to Dallas Tuesday after dinner and we parked at the stalls under a big roof like we had done before. Herb, Joe, and I put locks on the stalls we would use. I told Herb he could use Cody to ride in the Grand Entry. I would use Toby. He said he liked that. He would take care of Cody like he was his. The next morning, Harley and his wife drove up. We all waved them over and helped them park next to us. Harley and his wife looked at that roan horse and asked how much I wanted for it. I told them $2500. They could go ahead and use him and they could pay me at the end of the rodeo. They liked that.

I entered the dogging and saddle bronc riding. There were cowboys from everywhere. Some world champions and some were former world champions. There were two rodeos a day for all of October. I mounted a lot of cowboys in the dogging. They all made money on our team. We all helped each other in their events. I didn't win any 1st, 2nd, or 3rd. I did win enough 4th, 5th, and 6th to make money. Pam and I together made over $3500 all of October. Harley made enough to almost pay for the roan in the dogging alone. His wife made money in the barrel racing to finish paying for the roan horse. This made a good team for Harley and his wife. The rodeo ended on a Thursday night. Friday we all said our good-byes. We all said, "See you at Fort Worth!" I had told them we were not going to Denver as it was too cold. We got home Friday afternoon. Dub followed us home and brought the 4x10 trailer home. He sure liked having the trailer to sleep in. Saturday we rested and I told my folks about the Dallas rodeo. Tuesday we went to the Kirbyville sale. I told Porter all about the Dallas rodeo. We walked over to the four-acre place to look at the grass and calves. Porter had brought two more calves and had them on the grass also. He said I could buy one if I wanted. I told him sure we wanted one. I wrote him a check for one of the calves.

Wednesday morning Ed Brown drove up to the sale. Ed told Pam and me about a Ducks Unlimited Banquet in Jasper the next Saturday night. He had two tickets for us if we wanted to go. He and his wife were going. I told him sure and asked how much were the tickets. He said $5 each and we could go together if we wanted. We could leave our pickup at his place. Also they were having door prizes and a trip to Colorado for elk and deer hunting. I told him okay, we would be at his place about 6 p.m. Saturday. We worked the sale Wednesday. I bought a box of tack. It had halters, bridles, lead ropes, and a pair of spurs. We spent the night with Uncle Jud and Aunt Willie. I brought them up to date on all that had been happening. We went home Thursday.

Saturday we got to Ed Brown's place. He had bought a new Ford Ranch Wagon. We all went to Jasper in his new Ranch Wagon. We had our tickets and they took half and put the other half in the drawing. After supper, they held the drawing. Mrs. Brown's ticket was drawn. It was for four to go on a free hunt at Gunnison, Colorado. Mrs. Brown wanted us all to go. We talked all the way back about the trip. We needed to call and find out about the days of the hunt. We got to Ed's place and Pam and I went to Uncle Jud's and spent the night. Ed wanted us to come back about 9 a.m. so he could call Gunnison and find out more about the hunt. That day was the 10th of November. The ranch in Gunnison wanted us to come and hunt on the 20th, a Wednesday. He told us it would take about twenty hours straight to drive it. We needed to get there by noon Tuesday. We would need to leave Monday about noon. Ed told them we would be there.

Ed wanted us to all go in his new Ranch Wagon. We could take turns driving. I told him we had a 4 x 10 trailer all closed in; we could put a lot of stuff in it. Ed said we needed to take a lot of ice chests in case we got an elk. We all decided we would split everything fifty-fifty. I said why don't we use a bank deposit purse. We could put each a hundred dollars in the purse and buy gas and food with that. They liked that idea. Ed asked what gun I was going to use. He had a .270 rifle with a scope. I told him I would take my 20 gauge single barrel and use slugs to shoot and he said that should be big enough. I said that I would sight it in from 100-200-300 yards and see how much drop it had. We got back to Ed's place about 10 p.m. We drove back to Uncle Jud's place and spent the night. Sunday morning we drove home to Nederland. Monday morning we drove to E.C.'s pasture to sight the 20 gauge at 100 yards-200-300 yards. This way I figured I could hit anything and have a clean shot.

We came home and started planning for the trip to Colorado. We gathered all the ice chests we had and my folk's too. We put a piece of carpet in the trailer that covered all the floor then put all the ice chests in and two tarps to cover the ice chests. We worked the sale Wednesday and talked to Ed and Porter. I told Ed that we would be at his place Monday morning early. We spent the night at Uncle Jud's. We looked at Jake and he seemed to like it there on the farm. I helped Uncle Jud pull that wolf tooth. Then we went home to Nederland. Sunday we hooked the 4 x 10 trailer to Ed's new Ranch Wagon and left for Colorado. Ed and I did the driving. We decided to change drivers about every 2 ½ -3 hours. We drove non-stop and got to Gunnison, Colorado about 22 hours later (about noon on Tuesday). A fellow named Jim Stone met us and led us to the ranch. He and his wife ran the ranch for his uncle and his uncle's wife (the Randalls). We ate dinner before we got there. Jim wanted to know if we had ever ridden mules or horses. Ed told him we had ridden a bit. Jim smiled real big and said every time his guests say that they have ridden a little, they have never ridden at all or they are very good riders. I told him Ed and his wife had a pair of red mules that they have been riding lots of times, 6-10 hours a day and my wife had a red gaited mule and I had a gray gaited mule and we had ridden many hours together. Jim said he had a feeling we were good riders.

Then Jim asked our names and addresses for their records. After he got all that for his records he got a map of the place we were to hunt. He asked about what kind of guns we had brought. Ed told him he had a .270 rifle with a 3X9 scope. I told him I would use my 20 gauge single barrel and would use slugs. I had shot it at 100-200 and 300 yards. He looked at me and smiled but didn't say a word. Jim said there was a cabin where we were going to hunt. He would take us there on mules and we would stay in the cabin. He would show us some deer and elk blinds and then he would check on us at noon each day. In a little while Jim said that we should all go to the mule barn. Jim started to saddle the mules, so we all got the saddles and started to saddle mules also. Jim led the way to the cabin. First, he took us all to the deer and elk blinds. Jim showed me a cave in a draw. It was about six feet higher than the draw. There was a bunch of trees about 100x100 feet. Jim told me that this was a good place to hunt. No one had hunted from this spot all season. I got off my mule and walked up a ledge to the cave. It was about seven feet high, eight feet wide, and ten feet deep. I liked it real well since I would be out of the weather. Then Jim took us to the blind that Ed was to use. It was up on a derrick about fifteen feet high all closed in with windows. Ed got off his mule and climbed up and looked inside and said it was good. Jim told us we would have to walk to these places to hunt from. If we rode the mules and tied them they would bray all the time and mess up the hunt.

Then Jim took us back by the cave and turned left and went about two hundred yards to the cabin and barn combination. On one side was a fifty-foot cabin with a bedroom on each end and a kitchen in the middle. Then a hallway about 16x50 and four stalls on the other side. Jim told us he would be back about noon the next day. He told us we could take one deer and one elk. If he heard us shoot he would come back on a four-wheeler with a trailer to haul our game on. We unloaded our mules, put our sleeping gear in our bedrooms and put the mules in the barn. The next morning Ed and I went to the places Jim had showed us. Mrs. Brown and Pam stayed in the cabin. I got in the cave before daylight and Ed got in his stand just at daylight. About 7:30 a.m. I was looking out the cave when I saw a mule deer slipping along real quiet. He stopped about a hundred feet from me. His head was behind a tree. I took aim at his chest right behind his front leg. I pulled the trigger and the buck fell right in his tracks. I could see the buck lying on the ground. I reloaded my 20-guage with another slug. I watched him for a few minutes, and then I eased down and walked up to him, watching his eyes. If he blinked, he was still alive. He did not blink so I eased up real slow. Just then I heard Ed shoot. I figured he had an elk. I took my small chain, about four-foot long, and chained the deer to a tree. In a little bit Pam and Mrs. Brown came walking up. Pam said that was the biggest deer she had ever seen. We could hear Jim on his four-wheeler coming our way. He came driving up pulling a 4x10 lowboy trailer. He said he had heard both of us shoot. He could tell the difference in the 20 gauge and the .270. He stopped and looked at the deer I had shot. I told him to go check on Ed. We would go back and saddle the mules, get all our stuff, and meet him right there. Jim said okay and left to go help Ed.

We went to the cabin, got all our things, saddled the mules and got back to the deer. Jim and Ed got there just as we rode up. Ed had ridden the trailer with the elk he shot. It was a nice young bull elk. Jim backed the trailer up about sixty feet to the deer. He had a piece of ¾ plywood about 2-foot by 8-foot. He had a chain on one end. We put the plywood on the ground close to the deer and rolled the deer over on to the plywood. Jim told us this way we would not bruise the meat. Jim had a crank winch on the trailer. He pulled the cable to the deer, put the cable on the chain and winched the plywood and deer on to the trailer. Jim got on the four-wheeler and went about twenty feet. When he looked back, the trailer and four-wheeler was just sitting, the tires on the four-wheeler were spinning.

I had not gotten on my mule yet. The four-wheeler and trailer were in about two inches of snow and mud. I walked to Pam and gave her my lead rope to hold my mule. Then I walked over to Jim and asked if he had any rope. Jim said yes but asked why I wanted it. I told him that I thought the mules could pull him out to solid ground. Jim said there was a box in the trailer with two ropes about thirty feet long. Jim got off the four-wheeler and got the two ropes. I took one and tied it to the front of the four-wheeler. Then I tied the other rope to the front of the four-wheeler on the other side. Jim said he didn't know if the mules would pull with a saddle. I told Jim that it was time they learned. I asked Jim to get on the four-wheeler and get ready. I handed one rope to Pam and told her to take two wraps on the saddle horn. I told Ed and his wife to get in front of us. Ed said that we didn't have any ropes. I told Ed, "Don't tell the mules that." I got on my mule and took two wraps on the saddle horn. I told Ed and his wife to get about eight feet in front of us. I told them when I hollered at my mule, for them to holler at their mules also. That way our mules will think all the mules would be pulling. Jim just looked at us and shook his head. We all got in front like a four up team. We all talked to our mules and Jim got on the four-wheeler. Pam and I had the only mules pulling, but our mules didn't know that. They pulled the four-wheeler and the trailer with the elk and deer on it. We pulled everything out of the mud and on to solid ground. When we stopped, Jim smiled and said, "Well, I learned something today."

Jim said he had to go around in order to stay on solid ground. We could cut through and it would be a short cut. We would all get to the house together. We all got back to headquarters together. Jim drove the four-wheeler and trailer in the hallway under two chain hoists. We unsaddled the mules and put them up. Jim's wife came out to see what we had. Jim put a chain around the horns of the elk and hoisted him up to skin him. Then he did the same for the deer. Ed helped Jim skin the elk. I started on the deer. Jim asked how we wanted the elk and deer processed. I told him we would split the elk and deer 50/50. We wanted the hindquarters on both the deer and the elk made into steaks and roasts as well as the back strap. All the rest could be ground up to hamburger meat in about two-pound packages. While we put the hindquarters up, Pam and Mrs. Brown started boning out the rest to be ground up. We packaged the hindquarters and put them in the walk-in cooler.

Pam and Mrs. Brown went to hel0 Mrs. Stone fix dinner. Mrs. Brown started making two apple cobblers. Pam started to make dirty rice. Pam gladly showed what she was making. Then Pam took two roast pans and started to make skillet bar-b-que venison. Well, Mrs. Stone wanted to know all about it. Pam gladly showed her. We got all the elk and deer meat finished, packaged and put in the iceboxes. We did not have enough ice chests. Jim said it didn't surprise him. Jim told us that happened all the time. He bought Styrofoam ice chests ten at a time just for times like this one. Ed asked how much the boxes were. Jim said the ice chests were $5 each. They were 18x18x3 feet with lids. Ed told Jim we wanted two of them. We packed all the boxes and put dry ice in with the meat. Jim told us the meat would hold 3 or 4 days in the boxes with dry ice. By now the women had dinner just about ready. Mrs. Brown had made four pans of cathead biscuits, four biscuits to a pan. Mrs. Stone asked if we always pitched in and helped like this. They had never had guests to help as much as we had helped. Ed told them we always help out whatever we were doing. Them Jim told us this was by far the best visit they had ever had. Mrs. Stone asked if it was okay to invite Jim's uncle and aunt to come eat dinner with us. We all said sure and told her to go get them.

Jim told us the Randalls were his aunt and uncle. They did not have any kids and they had already deeded the ranch to him. Jim said that he and his wife had two boys in college. His boys wanted to come back there and work on his ranch after college but he was not sure if the ranch could support all of them. I told Jim I knew of a plan and after dinner I would tell him about it. Just then Mrs. Stone and the Randalls walked up. They looked to be in their middle 80's, but got around real good. We all set down at the table to eat dinner. Jim was surprised with the skillet bar-b-que elk, dirty rice, and venison. After dinner I told Jim about the Starr ranch and their operation (I did not tell him where the ranch was at). I told them it was a good guest ranch and all about it. Jim said he was real glad to know all of this.

Mrs. Stone went to the kitchen and got four cat head biscuits. She put bar-b-que elk in the biscuit and sandwiches. She said we could eat these on the way home. We thanked them for everything. We left at 2 p.m. and headed for home. We traveled straight through and got back to Kirbyville about twenty hours later on Friday. We stopped at the butcher shop and put a lot of meat in the deep freezer. I kept Uncle Jud's ice chest with a lot of meat in it; also my folks' box and our box and Harry and Arlene's box. We then went to Ed's house and unloaded his meat. We all helped with it. Then we hooked the trailer up to the '47 pickup and Pam and I drove to Uncle Jud's farm. I got his ice chest and took it in the house. We spent the night with Uncle Jud and Aunt Willie. I told them all about the trip. Then Uncle Jud told us about a fellow that saw him with Little Jim pulling a two-wheel cart. He was spreading manure with a log. He stopped and asked if that whole rig was for sale. Uncle Jud told him I would probably sell it. He told him that he was looking for us to be home Saturday early. The man said he would be there about 8:30 a.m. Uncle Jud told him okay.

Saturday we got up early. I had Little Jim all harnessed up to the cart. The man and his wife drove up with another man with them. He introduced himself and his wife and the fellow. He asked if I would sell the rig, and how much. I told him yes, that the complete rig was $800.

He said okay, that he wanted it. He said he and his wife would drive it back to Jasper. The fellow with them would drive the pickup back. He would stay behind them and follow along. He asked if I would take a check. I told him sure and to make the check to Circle W Enterprises. He handed me the check and they all left for Jasper. Uncle Jud had told me about the city of Newton and wanted to talk to us about buying water at the gravel pit. I had told him good, that I was always around. We would be back up Wednesday to work the sale. We talked about what kind of deal to tell the mayor and city manager. Uncle Jud suggested not to sign a five-year contract, just one year at a time and not to furnish a water pump. If the pump goes out, they repair it. I told Uncle Jud thanks for his part. Then we headed for Nederland. We got home and I gave my folks back their ice chest with lots of elk and venison and told them all about the trip. After dinner Harry and Arlene came out. I got his ice chest with lots of meat in it. I asked Harry how the two carts were coming along. He said that one cart was finished and ready for the windshield. I told him to go ahead and start another one. I had sold Uncle Jud's cart and Little Jim. Harry said I was going to need some horses to pull carts. I said yes, I was already thinking about that. I told Harry that we had to go back to Kirbyville Wednesday morning to work the sale. Also the city manager and the mayor wanted to talk to us about the water at the gravel pit. When we got back from Kirbyville, I would check with the Starr ranch and see if they have some horses to pull the carts.

Monday morning I took the two-wheel cart and had a Plexiglas windshield put on it. I brought the cart back and Pam and I decided to go to Uncle Jud's Tuesday and take the two-wheel cart. We got there and Uncle Jud was glad to get a new cart. I told him I was going to check on getting some horses to pull the carts. We spent the night with Uncle Jud and went to the sale barn early Wednesday. The city manager and the mayor drove up to talk about buying water from the gravel pit. We talked a while and then I told them I wanted one cent a gallon. They would put their pump house on the lake and put the water line down. They acted like one cent a gallon was too high. They said they would present the deal to the commissioners and get back to me. I told them okay.

Uncle Jud was standing there and heard the whole deal. I also told them I would have a lawyer go over the contract. It would have to be a one-year contract. The city fellows said they really wanted a five-year deal at the time. Well, I said taxes and cost of living goes up every year, so I could not take a five-year deal. They said they could see what I was thinking and would present this to the board as well. I told them I would b here the next Wednesday. They said okay and left. We worked the sale and told Uncle Jud we were going to Nederland. We would check on some horses and might be back Sunday evening and leave from there Monday; I thought it would be about an hour quicker drive. He said okay and he would see us Sunday. I told Uncle Jud we would bring horses back by Newton.

Thursday Pam and I rode Gray Boy and Star, our gaited mules. We rode to the fresh water canal and headed back. As we rode along, Dub, the horse shoer, came by just as we got home. When we got home Dub asked about the 4x10 trailer. He wanted to buy it so he could sleep in it at Fort Worth. I told him I would take $400 for the trailer. Also I was planning on getting some more horses and we could trade out hoof trimming. Dub liked that idea and asked when he could start. I told him he could trim everything there. I would let him know when I bought some more horses. Dub said he would trim some that day and do some more the next day. We worked Chip on barrels. We decided that Chip was a faster horse on barrels than Sandy. Pam thought she would use Chip at the Fort Worth rodeo. Sandy was a good all-around horse and I could use him for a pick-up horse. Sunday I called the Starr ranch about some horses to pull carts. Bill wanted us to come on that evening and spend the night and go back home Monday. I told him okay, we should be there about 3 or 4 p.m. We hooked the 16-foot stock trailers to the ¾ ton headed for the Starr ranch. Bill Starr was glad to see us. We picked four sorrel horses that would work and ride. They were ¾ Welsh and ¼ Belgian and 53" to 55" tall. I asked Bill how much and he told me $150 each. I wrote him a check on the Circle W account.

Monday morning we left out early. We stopped in Livingston at the saddle shop. He had two saddles that I liked for $50 each. We got to Uncle Jud's about noon. I told Uncle Jud that I would leave the horses with him and go to Nederland. He said they would be company to Tater, the gaited horse. Also there was lots of green oats for them to eat. We looked at Jake and he was already looking better. We stayed at uncle

Jud's and rode the new horses. We went to the sale Tuesday evening and tagged a few cows. Porter was there and he told us the steers could not keep up with the oats on the feed lot. He thought we should watch for two more steers to put with the others. Thursday we went home. Friday morning about 7 a.m. the phone rang, it was Tom Parker at Bleakwood. He told me that there was a fellow there wanting a pair of work horses. I told him I had four good sorrel horses that would work and ride, and asked when he wanted to look at them. Tom told me as soon as possible and that he had the money and the man was there at his store. I told him we were leaving right then and we should be there about 9 or so. We would be driving a maroon '47 pickup. Tom said he would be waiting there at his store. We got there a little before 9 a.m.

Tom introduced us to Tobe Garrett. He was driving a 1946 two-door sedan Ford car. Tobe told us he had brought the old McCoy place about two miles south of Parker's Store. It was a house and sixty acres. He wanted a couple of horses to farm with. He had gotten out of the army about a year before and had been looking for a farm to live on. He said he was married but she had left him while he was overseas. Now he was divorced and it was just him, no kids. I told him I had four good horses that would work and ride. He told me he would need a wagon also, that he was not going to keep the car. I asked him to follow us to the farm just past Newton. We got to Uncle Jud's and showed him the four sorrel horses. I told him we could hook them up to a two-wheel cart and try them out. I got on the cart with him and told him the advantages about a cart. It would be a lot easier to get on than a wagon, it had a windshield and a roof, and it had a storage box at our feet and another behind the seat. Then I told him how we farm with carts and all he could do with a cart. Tobe said that he had changed his mind about a wagon. I told him we could pull a wagon with a cart.

Tobe asked how much for the two 54-ince horses, collars, and cart and asked it I would take the 1946 car in trade. I told Tobe the wheel cart was $400, the horses and collars were 4450 each ($900), totaling $1300. I would allow $200 for the car leaving a balance of $1100. He said he knew the car was not much and that he knew the rig was the best that he had ever seen. I told him I sold a rig like it for the same price. He said he wanted the rig and asked if I would take a check on the Newton bank. I told him sure; I used the Newton bank also. We went to the bank and put the car title in my name. He wrote me a check for the rig, and I deposited the check in the Circle W account. We went back to Uncle Jud's and I told him Pam and I would ride the gaited gray donkeys along with him to his farm to see that he got home okay. Then Tobe got his 410 shotgun out of the car and put it in the box in the cart. We saddled the gaited donkeys and rode all the way to his farm. Tobe thanked us and asked us to stop by anytime and I told him to do the same. I told him we were going to build a rubber car tired wagon that we like to keep one in stock. Tobe said he would probably want the wagon to haul corn with. We rode the gaited donkeys back to Uncle Jud's. I asked Pam if she wanted to drive the car or the pickup. She told me she liked pickups and I could drive the car. We stopped in Newton and filled the car and pickup with gas. We both drove 55 to 60 miles per hour. I filled up again in Nederland and the car and the truck got 20 miles per gallon. We got home and put the car under the shed.

Pam and I drove the pickup to the wrecking yard to see what they had for tires that would fir the 1946 Ford 2-door sedan. He had four tires and wheels almost new for $10 each. I bought all four and put them in the pickup. Then he showed us the wrecked '48 2-door sedan that the tires came from. The front seat was in real good condition. The front seat in the '46 was about worn out, so I bought this also. We went back by an auto parts store and bought spark plugs, points and condenser, about six quarts of oil and a filter for the '46 sedan. We went home and I changed the oil and the filter. I was changing the plugs when Harry and Arlene drove up. I told them all that had been happening and how we got the '46 sedan. Harry put the points and condenser in and set the timing, he said he likes fixing cars. Saturday we all put the tires on the car. Harry asked what plans I had for the '46 car. I told him I thought about having it painted. The car needed a paint job. Harry then asked if I would sell them the car and for how much. He said that if Arlene had a car she would drive to work, to the store, and other things. I told him I would have about $500 by the time I had it painted and other things. He could trade out the car with labor on carts. Also he could go ahead and put the title in his name. I was thinking about having maroon paint if they liked it or whatever color they wanted. We could take it to the paint and body shop in the morning. Arlene said she liked maroon just fine. Harry and Arlene drove the car and we followed to the paint and body shop. The shop man looked at the car and the dents it had. He told me it would be $250 for the paint and body work and it would be ready Friday evening. I told him okay and we would see him Friday.

We worked on carts all week. There was no sale Wednesday, as they were closed for Christmas. Friday evening after Harry and Arlene got off work, we all went to the paint and body shop. We drove up and the Ford sedan was parked out front. We were all surprised at how good it looked. Harry and Arlene drove the car back home. We all put the good seat in the car. We worked on carts all weekend. Monday I called Big T Trailers, and I told him I had sold the silver 16-foot stock trailer and I needed some four-foot axles to build a two-wheel cart. He told me had just talked to the man that makes the axles. He told him that he was going to have to increase the price on axles because the material was costing more, but he could order more axles before the price went up.

Mr. T told me that he had two trailers already built and he would paint them the color I wanted. The trailers would still be $800 each. I told Mr. T that I wanted both trailers and to paint them both silver. Then I asked about four-foot axles, and he told me again those four-foot axles would go up in price, but that he still had sixteen four-foot axles he would let go if I wanted them for $60 each. I told him I wanted all sixteen axles and to put them in one of the trailers. I asked him when he could deliver the trailer to my place in Nederland. Mr. T said he could deliver the trailers January 6th, with the axles inside. I told Mr. T that would be fine on the delivery. Pam and I kept working with the barrel and dogging teams, getting them ready for Fort Worth. Well, I wonder what 1951 would be like, 1950 was a good year. Oh well, time will tell.